4

QUEST FOR A LORD

Grace Fairweather is determined to find the father of her friend's orphaned son in order to give him a good start in life. She travels to London in search of Lord P — the name whispered by her friend Kathy with her dying breath. There she meets handsome, disillusioned rake Lord Jaspar Ede, and charming, golden-haired Richard Mercury, both of whom seek her love. But first she must navigate her way through the snares of London, which can spell ruin for an unwary girl . . .

Books by Sara Judge
in the Linford Romance Library:

THE GYPSY'S RETURN
LUCIFER'S HOLD
TUDOR STAR
THE BLOODSTONE RING
THE ORANGE MISTRESS
TABITHA'S REVENGE

SARA JUDGE

QUEST FOR
A LORD

Complete and Unabridged

LINFORD
Leicester

First published in Great Britain in 1985 by
Robert Hale Limited
London

First Linford Edition
published 2010
by arrangement with
Robert Hale Limited
London

British Library CIP Data

Judge, Sara.
    Quest for a lord. - -
(Linford romance library)
1. Paternity- -Fiction. 2. Aristocracy
(Social class)- -England- -London- -
Fiction. 3. Love stories. 4. Large type books.
I. Title II. Series
823.9'14–dc22

ISBN 978–1–84782–985–6

Published by
F. A. Thorpe (Publishing)
Anstey, Leicestershire

Set by Words & Graphics Ltd.
Anstey, Leicestershire
Printed and bound in Great Britain by
T. J. International Ltd., Padstow, Cornwall
This book is printed on acid-free paper

TO SANDRA

1

On the 4th March, 1829 Grace Fairweather caught the stage coach to London. Her father did not come to see her safely away on her journey, and Grace wished that she did not have to leave him in such a black and unforgiving mood. But she had made a promise to her friend, and a death-bed vow must be kept.

Grace adjusted her bonnet over her red hair, pulled her cloak more firmly around her, and tried to doze as the coach lumbered on its way towards the great city. Joan, the wet nurse, sat beside her, a square, shabby figure in her brown skirt and shawl, and Sammy, warmly wrapped, lay against her shoulder.

The interior of the coach smelt of old straw and, despite the presence of four other occupants, was bitterly cold. Still, they had been fortunate to gain seats inside, Grace realised. Only the other week she had heard in the village of a woman and her child who had been forced to travel outside, and who had been found dead of exposure on the coach's arrival in London. Grace shivered at the thought and pressed closer to Joan for warmth.

At the Golden Cross Inn they were put down and Grace asked advice from a friendly-faced maid at the coaching house.

'We are looking for clean lodgings,' she said. 'Not too luxurious, for we have not the money, but the rooms must be comfortable enough for ourselves and the baby.'

The girl directed them to a lodging house in Cecil Street, off the Strand, where Grace was shown three neat little rooms which seemed clean enough. Mrs Luce, who owned the establishment, appeared a respectable body, and Grace parted with one of her precious coins to cover two weeks' lodging. Then she told Joan to unpack and settle the baby, whilst she went out in search of food.

It was late afternoon and all the shops were open, so Grace purchased bread and cheese, tea and sugar, and took them back to the house with a light heart.

Their sitting-room, which lay between the two bedrooms on the first floor, possessed a horse-hair couch, a round table by the window with two chairs drawn up to it, and a dresser which sported cups and saucers of many different colours and designs. There was nothing pretty in any of the rooms, but Grace was used to stark necessity in the Vicarage at home, and Joan Crump looked upon the lodgings as if they were a palace. There was a small range in the sitting-room on which Joan could cook, and the price of coal was included in the rent.

Grace gave a contented sigh as she cuddled Sammy to her, and Joan made tea. They were warm and comfortable, and all that remained was for her to locate Lord P. She would begin the search on the very next day.

Grace spent a restless night for she was unaccustomed to noise, and the sounds of carriage wheels on the cobbles beneath her window, and the shouts and chatter of passing folk, seemed to go on until well after midnight. Then, when she finally fell asleep, the clamour began again at dawn.

In the morning she kissed Sammy's rosy face and told Joan not to stir from the rooms until she returned, for she was fearful that the girl would lose herself if she ventured out. Then Grace wrapped her shawl about her shoulders, adjusted her bonnet, and went out to begin her quest.

Her gown was of a shabby blue velvet, but Joan had given it a good brushing the night before, and with her grey spun shawl, black boots well polished, and black mittens, she felt reasonably well clad and able to face whatever Fate held in store for her.

Grace was pale from her disturbed night but there was only a small, fly-spotted mirror in her room, and apart from seeing that her bonnet was straight, and that all her hair was tucked firmly away beneath it, she had paid no further attention to her countenance. Thus she did not realise that her pallor accentuated her large grey eyes, and that her lashes appeared very black against her white skin. Grace knew only that she was neat and tidy and what her father would describe as presentable.

The first thing she was going to do was to find the Theatre Royal in Drury Lane. This was where she knew Kathy had been in her youth, and it seemed as good a place to start as any.

The only information she had been able to glean from Kathy before she died was the fact that Sammy's father was a wealthy man, and that he was titled, and that his name began with a P.

Granny Lang, to whom her friend had returned, mortally sick, with her baby son, knew nothing more.

'Kathy was a silly girl, running off like that to make her fortune on the stage. And now she's suffered from that daft notion. She told me nothing, Grace, only called for you with her dying breath.'

Grace had run down to Granny Lang's cottage on that stormy night of Kathy's return, but her childhood friend had been beyond help. She had whispered hoarsely, begging Grace to care for her son, and to find his father. But her words had been unclear, and Kathy had died before Grace could find out the name of the boy's father.

Mrs Luce gave her a strange look when Grace asked directions to the theatre, but said nothing more than,

'Go straight along the Strand, dearie, then turn left at the top.'

Grace would have liked to dawdle, to have looked in at all the enticing wares in the shop fronts, and to have stared at the people and the horse-drawn vehicles in the busy thoroughfare. But she hurried her steps, knowing that time was important. After asking the way once more, she found herself outside the theatre and was directed to the stage door at the rear of the building.

Maybe there would be somebody here who remembered Kathy? Someone who might be able to direct her to the home of Lord P, or at least furnish her with his correct name? But she would have to ask tactfully. Grace did not know in what circumstances her friend had left the theatre world, nor where she had lived during her confinement. And people could be cruel. Kathy's memory was precious to her, and she did not want to hear unkind remarks about the girl whom she had genuinely loved.

Just inside the door sat an old man, writing laboriously at a little table before him.

'Good morning,' said Grace, 'could

you please tell me — '

'What's your name?' he interrupted, sucking at his teeth and regarding her in an unfriendly manner.

'Grace Fairweather,' she replied, surprised by his abrupt tone. 'I wondered if — '

'Straight up them stairs and turn left at the top,' he said, 'somebody'll see to you there.'

'Oh.' She stared, perplexed, but his head lowered again over the table and he continued with his writing.

Grace shrugged, lifted her skirts, and climbed the short flight of steps before her. She could hear a murmur of voices at the end of the passage, and made her way hesitantly towards the sound.

A young man poked his head round the corner ahead and saw her.

'Here's another,' he called over his shoulder, 'come on, miss, you're late.'

He put out his hand, grabbed her arm, and pulled her between pieces of scenery out onto the wooden boards of the stage.

A group of some twenty other girls stood there, chattering and whispering, touching their hair and their collars with nervous, self-conscious gestures.

'Take your bonnet off,' ordered the young man. And, scarcely aware of what she was doing, Grace obeyed him. 'That's it — now everybody, please face the front.'

Grace turned with the others, blinking in the harsh glare from the gas lamps, staring with widened eyes into the shadowy depths before her. Dear heavens, here she was, Grace Fairweather, standing in the middle of a London stage, surrounded by strangers, and feeling extremely foolish. What *would* her father think of such behaviour?

'Thank you, ladies,' said a voice from the blackness before them. 'We are only looking for six young ladies for walk-on parts in this production, so I am afraid many of you will be disappointed.' There was a whispered conversation and then the same voice said, 'Right, then we are agreed. I'm coming up.'

At the far corner of the stage a figure appeared, bounding up out of the darkness, pushing aside the heavy curtains which were draped at both sides of the stage, and leaping on to the boards. He moved forward with a smile and spoke to a small group of girls some distance from Grace.

Around her, other females pushed and argued and cursed, some quite loudly and aggressively, making Grace shiver with trepidation. They were not nice girls, she could tell that, and some of the words they were using were unknown to her, but she felt her face burn with shame because she knew that they were impolite.

Grace turned away, wishing to be gone from such company, wondering how Kathy had managed to exist in these surroundings. But as she started to leave the stage, she felt a hand on her shoulder and the man stood before her, smiling.

'You, too,' he said. 'May I have your

name and address, please?'

He was tall, fair-haired and rosy-cheeked, and looked both clean and kind so she was not afraid. But she was disconcerted.

'Me?' she queried. 'I'm afraid I do not understand. Why do you want to know where I live?'

'Because you have been chosen to appear in my play,' he answered, an amused expression on his boyish face. 'Is that not the reason you came to this audition?'

'Audition?' Grace's eyes widened and she twisted the ribbons of her bonnet between her fingers. 'I do not know what you mean, sir. I am newly come from the country and am on an errand for a friend. A Miss Katharine Lang. Did you know her?'

The young man gaped, staring at her in astonishment as the rest of the girls passed them on their way out of the theatre.

'What is going on here, Crispin? We haven't all day, you know.' A deep voice

11

spoke behind them, and the young man swung round to face the newcomer.

'Quite the oddest thing, my dear Ede. This young lady seems to have wandered in here by mistake.' He let out a burst of laughter. 'She doesn't appear to know what an audition is!'

Grace looked up into the dark frowning countenance of a very tall, most elegantly attired gentleman. She curtseyed in some confusion.

The man wore a long coat of a deep rich brown, and beneath it Grace could see a fine embroidered waistcoat. His tight fitting trousers were cream-coloured, strapped beneath polished brown boots. His cravat was of a pale yellow silk and he carried a gold-topped cane in one long-fingered hand.

'What is your name, child?' asked the young man called Crispin.

'Grace Fairweather,' she said.

'Then, Ede, may I present Miss Grace Fairweather to your lordship,' said Crispin gravely, 'and Grace, this is Lord Jaspar Ede.'

A lord! Grace felt a thrill of excitement run through her body as the man bowed gracefully over her hand. If he were a lord he would certainly know of Lord P and she had only to become acquainted with him, then all her problems would be over.

Grace stared up at his lordship. His eyes, beneath very black brows, were hazel-coloured, with more gold in them than brown, and his hair was thick and dark and inclined to curl. His mouth was straight, rather grim looking, and his nose was straight and strong. Lord Jaspar Ede did not look as if he smiled readily, but Grace was not perturbed by this fact, being so used to her father's tetchiness. But she had never met a lord before, so she gazed at him for some time, unaware that her childlike interest was intensely provocative to his lordship's jaded eyes.

'Did you know a Katharine Lang, sir? A young girl from the country, like me, but very pretty, and dark-haired? She might have come here two or three years ago?'

Slowly his lordship shook his head, scarcely hearing what she was saying, bemused by her clear eyes, her sweet mouth, and wonderful soft complexion, which was unmarked by paint or grime.

'We have a goddess here, Crispin,' he remarked softly, 'what remarkable good fortune. And that hair!' He stretched out his hand and touched her hair, awed by its glorious colour. 'Can you see that beneath the lights? And with her dressed in black — in the Ballroom scene? With her eyes and mouth emphasised, and well-laced — ' he stepped back, looking at her figure with appreciation. 'She'll stun 'em, Crispin, be the find of the season. Can you act, my dear?'

'Act?' Grace's eyes widened in shock. 'Oh, dearie me, no, sir! Kathy was the actress and I have no such pretensions. I am merely here on an errand and — '

'All right, all right.' Lord Jaspar held up his hand impatiently. 'She'll need plenty of rehearsing.' He turned to Crispin. 'Write in a few more lines, the voice is not bad. Develop the plot, my dear fellow, this is a rarity which must be shown off. Get Lottie to coach her, she must not let us down, and with those looks she is certain to succeed.'

'What about Fanny Kelly?' said Crispin. 'I hear she can take more pupils at that school of hers. Maybe she could spare a few hours for coaching?'

'Admirable,' answered his lordship, 'see to it at once.'

2

Grace walked back to her lodgings in a daze. She had signed a piece of paper, agreed to appear in Crispin Mellish's new play, entitled *The Countess From Crewe*, and would soon be receiving a regular wage. She must send word to her father at once, but he was not going to like what he heard, of that she was certain.

Still, Grace consoled herself, she would be earning money for herself and Sammy and Joan and, if they lived carefully, she would even be able to send money home to her father, which should appease his wrath somewhat. Also, being so involved in theatre life, she would surely come across somebody who had known Kathy, and would probably also learn the whereabouts of Lord P before very long.

Grace had been shown the dressing-rooms by the young man who had first met her in the passage. His name was Robin Mark, and he was the stage manager. Her dressing-room was right at the top of the building, up three flights of stairs, and was a small, draughty room which she was to share with the five other girls.

She was introduced to Mrs Bundle, the dresser, who was in charge of all the costumes for the girls, and her assistant, Violet Hill. The dresser appeared a kindly, comfortable old body and Grace determined to ask her about Kathy the moment she got the chance. But that first morning there was no time for chatter, she had been given Miss Fanny Kelly's address in Dean Street, and had been told to report to her at No 73 that very afternoon.

When Grace arrived back at the lodging-house, she told a curious Joan about her adventures, played with Sammy for a short time before his nap, wrote a hurried letter to her father, ate a meal of bread and cheese, then went forth to Dean Street.

Miss Kelly was a successful actress who wished to raise the status of her profession by training young girls for the stage in proper surroundings.

'I have been most fortunate in my life,' she told Grace, 'but too many females are at the mercy of unscrupulous touring managers, who make use of the girls *in all sorts of ways.* Then they discard them, thus giving our profession a bad reputation.'

Miss Kelly was not beautiful, indeed, she was almost plain with somewhat large, flat features. But her light blue eyes were full of merriment and she smiled readily. Grace liked her and listened eagerly to her instructions.

'The Lane is my favourite theatre,' Miss Kelly told her, 'and you are lucky to be appearing there. Of course, it is not the place I once knew, for Old Drury burnt down in the February of 1809 and we had to transfer to the Lyceum. But thank heavens it was rebuilt in time and now the Theatre Royal is more splendid than before.'

Fanny Kelly taught Grace how to speak, and how to move for the stage, and she also showed her how to apply greasepaint to her face so that her features could be easily discernible from the back of the auditorium.

For the rest of that week Grace visited Miss Kelly every day and on the Friday she found Lord Ede standing outside the building with his carriage waiting in the street behind him.

'It is time you and I became better acquainted, Miss — er — what did you say your name was?' He peered down at her from his great height.

'Grace Fairweather.'

'Then, Miss Fairweather, I intend taking you out for a meal. Don't suppose you are eating properly in those lodgings of yours.'

'How do you know about my lodgings?' Grace stared up at him. 'And they are quite comfortable, thank you, sir. Joan and I are managing well.'

'Who is Joan?' Lord Jaspar assisted her into his carriage and settled himself beside her as the wheels began to roll.

'She is — she is my maid.' Nobody was to be told about Sammy until she had found Lord P. If Kathy had told anyone about her predicament then those friends would surely make themselves known to Grace when she encountered them. But she would not have Kathy's misfortune gossiped about by all and sundry. So the baby would remain a secret for the time being.

'Father said I was not to travel to London on my own, so I brought Joan with me. And we must go by Cecil Street now, if you please, sir, so I can tell Joan I won't be home until later. She will worry, else.'

His lordship tapped on the roof of the carriage with his gold-tipped cane, and when the driver stopped the horses, Lord Jaspar put his head out of the window and gave the man instructions. Then they were on their way again and her companion turned to look down at Grace.

'George will deliver your message

once he has left us at our eating house. How wise of your father to send you with a chaperone, Miss Grace. You have a fair way to walk from your lodgings to the Lane, and then to Miss Kelly's every afternoon. You should take your maid with you, it is not sensible to walk the streets unattended.'

Grace blushed. 'Joan would be very bored sitting about waiting for me,' she said quickly, 'and I am quite safe, I assure you, sir. I walk swiftly, you see, and do not gaze about me or look anywhere save straight ahead.'

His lordship grunted but made no reply.

'Where are we going, sir? I have not been to this part of the city before.'

Grace was peering out of the window, amazed at the grand buildings, and the expensive looking shops, and the elegantly attired people who were parading in the wide thoroughfare. It was very different to the humble streets around the theatre, and to Cecil Street where she lodged with Mrs Luce.

'We are going to a particular haunt of mine,' replied Lord Jaspar, 'where the food is passable, the wine excellent, and where privacy is assured. After that I think some shopping would not go amiss. You appear to be wearing the same gown which you wore on Monday.'

Grace felt her cheeks flame and she turned her attention away from the window towards his lordship's expressionless face.

'Indeed, it is the same gown, sir, but 'tis brushed and clean. Although I am only a poor girl from a country vicarage, it is considered bad manners to make personal remarks about a lady's appearance, where I come from. Especially if those remarks are derogatory.' Her grey eyes flashed and her chin tilted alarmingly. 'I may not possess much money but it is not a crime to be poor, and I consider good manners and kindness to be of more value than bodily apparel and costly jewels.'

'Well said, young lady.' Lord Jaspar

looked amused by her outburst. 'So your father is a parson? I wonder what he will say to his daughter becoming an actress?'

Grace looked uncomfortable, her anger forgotten. 'I have written to tell him. He will not be pleased, I fear.'

His lordship shrugged. 'You are no longer a child, Miss Grace, and must do as you please. But if you are to become a famous young lady you must not appear dowdy.'

'I have no intention of becoming a famous actress,' Grace replied quickly. 'I have agreed to take part in Mr Mellish's play because it is a means of earning money, and because it suits my purpose. But the moment I have achieved my aim and the play has finished its run, I shall depart for the country and live a more normal life again.'

'Is life in London not normal?' Lord Jaspar Ede looked puzzled.

'Indeed not. It is all so artificial. All that I learn from Miss Kelly is affected and insincere. I have to speak slowly and pronounce each word clearly; no ordinary person would ever speak in such a stilted way. And the movements and postures are so — so obvious! I have entered a world of vanity and make-believe and I know my father would not approve.'

'But so long as *you* do not change and realise the reason for all this play-acting, that it is simply to amuse and entertain an audience, then surely it does not matter a jot?'

'So long as I do not change,' she echoed soberly. 'But for how long can one live a lie and not be affected by it?'

'That depends on how long it will take you to achieve your aim,' he replied. 'Perhaps you will escape in time. And Fanny Kelly is a most sincere and sensible female. She has not been adversely affected by her stage suc-cesses.'

'No,' Grace admitted, 'but then Miss Kelly is no ordinary woman.'

'Ah, the 'divine plain face',' remarked

Ede. 'Charles Lamb found her totally fascinating, and she was, and is, rather special. But perhaps you, too, will remain unspoilt, Miss Grace. Tell me, what is this aim of yours?'

Grace shifted on her seat. 'I am seeking anyone who knew a Miss Katharine Lang. Did you know her, sir? She would have come to London about three years ago?'

His Lordship shook his head. 'Never heard of her. Ah, here we are, young lady, now let us partake of refreshment and leave life's perplexities behind us for a few brief moments.'

As Lord Jaspar followed Grace into the restaurant where they were to dine, and the head waiter led them to the table which was always reserved for him, he admired the girl's neat figure, the erect carriage of her small head, and the seductive sway of her skirts, faded and unfashionable though they were.

It was a long time since he had been so taken by a young female. His senses were blurred, his mind dulled, by years of hard living and self satisfaction. Lord Jaspar had lost faith in people, and particularly in the weaker sex. They were all whores at heart and gave themselves to him with eager lust. His lordship was a confirmed bachelor, and a sadly disillusioned man. He wondered how long it would be before this pure little girl from a country vicarage fell into his arms.

Grace was entranced by the meal and by the sumptuous surroundings. There were chandeliers overhead, and a deep red carpet upon the floor, and many fashionably dressed folk sitting at small tables all round the large room. The waiters were instantly attentive, with swift deft movements, and plate after plate of unknown delicacies was placed before her. She could not face the oysters, but found the caviare interesting, the grouse delicious, and the roast beef better than any she had tasted before.

Grace had no knowledge of wine, but Lord Jaspar plied her with the chilled, delicately fragrant liquid, and she announced that she liked the taste very much indeed.

Then she smiled and let out a sigh. 'I must not let all this excitement go to my head,' she said, selecting a peach from the silver platter which was held out to her. 'It is a little like acting — frivolous, enchanting, but a totally unreal world.'

Lord Ede was silent, watching her every move and expression, enjoying the sight of her innocent pleasure.

'Do you write plays, sir?'

He smiled. 'Indeed, no, I have no talent for it. I supply the money for various productions, Miss Grace, and young Crispin is a protégé of mine. I believe him to be both intelligent and witty, and as his last play was considered a success, we are hopeful that *The Countess From Crewe* will also do well with London audiences.'

'Do many of your friends also have an interest in the theatre? I have heard that Lord P — ' Grace shook her head and put a hand to her brow. 'Dearie me, I have forgotten his name. Do you happen to know of a lord with a name beginning with P?' she asked innocently.

Lord Jaspar Ede frowned. 'Pridmont?'

'That might be it. Do you know him well, sir? Does he live in London?'

'I know him and he lives in Cavendish Square. But how do *you* know him, Miss Grace?' His lordship's face was cold and she thought that he looked rather angry.

'I heard of him from my friend and I wish to make contact with him.'

'Where is this friend of yours now?' Ede asked thoughtfully.

Grace hesitated. She did not wish to lie, but Kathy and her secret must be kept hidden until she had discovered if Lord Pridmont was really Sammy's father. 'She lives back home in our village,' said Grace carefully, 'and she once worked in the theatre, I believe. But she is ill at present and could not accompany me. I very much want to meet Lord Pridmont, because he may be the man I am seeking, and if so, I have a message for him.'

'Pridmont is not the sort of man with whom you should associate,' said Lord Jaspar, 'and I am surprised that your friend knew a man like that.'

'But I must see him,' insisted Grace. After all, she had promised.

'Then it will not be by my arranging,' answered his lordship curtly. 'Come, we have some shopping to do. Let us think of pleasant matters, and I refuse to see you one more day in that abominable worn-out velvet.'

'But I cannot go shopping!' cried Grace, as he began to usher her from the room, surrounded by bowing waiters, 'I have no money with me.'

'No matter. I shall pay for whatever you need.' Lord Jaspar pushed her before him out on to the pavement, ignoring her protests.

'I cannot accept presents from you, 'twould be most unseemly. I have another gown at home, sir, and will make sure to wear it tomorrow.'

'My dear young lady, two gowns are not enough, and if your other creation is of the same material and design as that present concoction, you may give them both to your maid.'

Ede bundled her up into his waiting carriage, spoke a few words to the driver, and they were off before Grace could fully gather her wits.

Despite her objections, Lord Jaspar Ede escorted Grace to a shop in Regent Street, at least, she *supposed* it to be a shop, it was quite unlike anything she had been in before, more like the private residence of somebody very rich.

She was whisked away into a boudoir of mirrors and gilt chairs, where she was measured and clucked over, and prodded and poked. Then her poor blue velvet was removed and she found herself being swathed in the most luxurious materials; taffetas and silks, tarlatans and satins.

To her surprise, Grace looked remarkably attractive when she viewed her reflection in one of the long mirrors, and oh, the beauty of those gowns!

Grace could not believe that it was herself, Parson Fairweather's daughter from Windhaven, who stood before the mirrors in such finery.

Then the black-clad lady, who seemed to be in charge of the establishment, accompanied her out into the other room and made her parade in one gown after another in front of Lord Ede. He sat, long-legged and rather ridiculous, perched on a spindly-backed chair which looked as if it would break beneath his weight at any moment.

His lordship smiled or frowned as Grace walked and twirled before him, her hair becoming increasingly untidy, hcr cheeks flushed, and her heart beating faster and faster beneath her laces.

Finally, two evening gowns were chosen, very tight-waisted and with heart-shaped bodices, one of white brocaded gauze, and the other of a very pale yellow organdie. Grace was astonished by the fullness of the sleeves which looked like enormous epaulettes, but the lady in charge told her that they were quite the thing.

Then his lordship decided on four day dresses, two of velvet, one in blue and the other in a soft lilac shade, and the others were made of chintz, in dove grey, and what the lady called 'violet de Parme'.

Grace was measured for new shoes, beautiful flat-heeled, square-toed creations, with black satin slippers for evening, and a matching black satin cloak. Lord Jaspar also ordered silk stockings, a grey cashmere shawl, and quantities of silk undergarments, trimmed with lace, which made Grace feel very embarrassed but which did not appear to disturb anyone else.

At the end of the exciting but rather exhausting business, Grace also found herself in possession of two wide-brimmed hats of leghorn, trimmed with field-flowers and dahlias, and a bonnet of grey velvet, topped by an enormous bow of matching gauze ribbon striped with silver. Then she was helped into her faded blue velvet again, and his lordship gave orders for the clothing to be delivered to Cecil Street the very next day.

'I shall never be able to repay you, sir,' Grace said breathlessly, as they sat once more in his carriage. 'And I should never have agreed to all these clothes, only you *were* so insistent!'

'You will find that I can be a most insistent fellow when there is something particular I desire,' drawled Lord Jaspar, lolling back in his corner of the carriage, a smile upon his firm lips. 'You surely could not admire a man who was a feeble nincompoop, now could you, my dear?'

Grace let out a spurt of laughter. 'Dear me, I don't know what's come over me, I really don't! But I have been acting quite out of character for these last few hours and you, why you, sir,

could never, *ever* be called a nincompoop!'

She giggled unrestrainedly, her grey
eyes brimming with laughter, her
cheeks flushed with merriment. She
looked extremely pretty and infinitely
desirable.

Lord Jaspar Ede crossed his legs,
allowing his body to lounge further
down on the seat, and turned his gaze
away from Grace's enchanting face.

She was the most entrancing female
he had met, and was so delightfully
natural. Could she be as innocent as
she looked? Had he at last met a girl
who was not out to catch a man? He
was not sure what to make of her, he
had never met anyone like her before,
but he was going to enjoy the hunt. For
once he forgot that he was bored with
everyone and everything in his life. He
found Grace Fairweather quite fascinating, and was determined to see a great
deal of her and discover if she was really
as demure and unworldly as she made
out.

'We shall charge the bill to the theatre,' he announced grandly, 'so you need have no guilty feelings as to the expense, and will thus be able to wear your new clothes with complete confidence and enjoyment.'

'Oh, I shall, I shall!' Grace turned towards him, her face sobering. 'I cannot tell you how grateful I am to you, sir, and how much I have enjoyed myself today. I know that I shall soon have to wake up from this pleasant dream, but for the moment it is all so wonderful, I thank you for making it happen to me.'

'It is my pleasure, dear young lady,' he answered softly, taking one of her hands and carrying it to his lips. 'And you are not to wake up yet, my beauty. There are more dreams yet to come.'

Grace smiled and withdrew her hand, feeling her heart begin to thud with uncomfortable force at his touch. Then the carriage slowed to a halt. 'Good day to you, sir, and a pleasant journey home.'

'Thank you,' Ede replied. 'I hope, one day, that you will come and see my home.'

'When I have time.' Grace glanced back over her shoulder as the coachman opened the door for her. 'This has been a special treat, but I doubt that there will be much time in the future. We begin rehearsing tomorrow.'

'There will be time,' he said, as she descended from the carriage. 'I shall see to that.'

Grace raised her hand in farewell, then turned and entered her lodging-house.

3

The dressing-room at the top of the Theatre Royal was small and, with six young women sharing it, space was limited. Grace wondered how they would all manage when performances began. How could they all put on their stage makeup when there were only two mirrors? And there would be scarcely room to struggle into their various costumes, although both Mrs Bundle and her assistant, Violet Hill, would be helping them.

As yet, the girls had not used their room, preferring to wait around in the wings, and behind the backdrop, never certain when they might be called for a scene. The rehearsals seemed to be one chaotic muddle, with Crispin Mellish arguing constantly with the producer, and the leading actor and actress having something to say about every problem which occurred.

Grace was only in three of the scenes, and had but a few lines to learn. But in the Ballroom scene, the hero, played by Lionel Chase, had to dance with her. There was some nice humour in the part when Grace had to explain that she was not the person he believed her to be, but merely standing in for her sister, who was indisposed.

For the rest of the time Grace and the other girls paraded as shoppers in the Street scene; as dancers in the Ballroom scene, where Grace had her big moment clad in a splendid black taffeta gown; and finally, they were all in the Palace scene, where Jemima Power, as the Countess, was presented at Court.

The girls spent most of their time sitting on upturned boxes, or standing about in small groups, grumbling and yawning. Grace was surprised at how dull the interior of the theatre looked in daytime. She saw row upon row of empty seats facing her, and there was no magic or excitement about the sets, or the backdrops, which appeared badly painted and tawdry at close quarters. She presumed that once the lamps were lit and an eager audience filled the space before her, and the players were made up and dressed in their lavish costumes, then the Theatre Royal would come alive. It needed the night-time, Grace thought, and the warmth of lights and enthusiastic people to make it function properly.

She knew that she was tired from all her lessons with Miss Kelly and the unending boredom of the rehearsals, but she had the uncomfortable feeling that the other girls did not like her. Grace confided her fears to Mrs Bundle, who had befriended her.

' 'Course they don't like you, ducks! Wot wiv Lord Ede being nice to you, and that part made special for you, all wrote in by Mr Crispin, they're jellus, that's wot. But don't let them get you down, Miss Grace.'

'Jealous — of me?' Then she

remembered the worn-down slippers of the others, and their torn shawls, and the ragged hems of their stained and dusty day dresses. Just like her, before his lordship bought her new clothes, she thought. No wonder they did not like her. Why should she receive gifts like that and they did not? 'I shall speak to Lord Jaspar and see if something cannot be done for the others,' she said to Mrs Bundle, that night before going home. 'He has plenty of money and could easily afford a new gown and a pair of slippers for each girl.'

'Don't be daft!' The old dresser stared at Grace in amazement. 'You hang on to wot you've got, but don't tempt Fate, dearie. Just 'cos 'e's rich and taken a fancy to you don't mean to say 'e's gotta be kind to every Jane and Dolly wot works 'ere. You'll make 'im cross, asking silly things like that, Miss Grace. They've got brains and bodies, same as you, and they can find themselves gentlemen like wot you done.'

'But I didn't *find* his lordship,' said Grace indignantly, 'he — he saw me at the audition, that's all.'

Mrs Bundle nodded. 'And admired your pretty face and got acquainted. Well, there'll be men a-plenty at the stage door on Opening night, and it's up to the girls to grab every opportunity wot comes their way, I says.'

Grace pondered. 'Do you know a Lord Pridmont?' she asked.

' 'Im! I should say so. Always out front when we've a new play on, looking for young girls, 'e is. Not a nice gentleman, miss. Now 'ow in the world did you 'ear of the likes of 'im, may I ask?'

'He knew a friend of mine, at least, I suppose it was him,' she said doubtfully. 'Kathy said his name began with a P and that he was a lord. I wonder if he *is* the right one? He doesn't sound pleasant at all.'

''E's not! And always with that pretty boy, running about taking messages for 'im. Now you be careful, Miss Grace, 'e

41

goes for the sweet and innocent ones, and 'e's a bad lot.'

'I shall have to see him, just once,' said Grace. 'Do you know his address, Mrs Bundle?'

'Cavendish Square, number thirty, I believe. But don't you go there on your own, miss. Make sure you take that nice Lord Ede with you. Now 'e's a *real* gentleman, if ever I saw one.'

He would not take her there, thought Grace. His lordship had made it quite clear that he would never help her to meet the man. She wondered again if this could possibly be Kathy's Lord P, and thus father of little Samuel. Why did everyone dislike him so much? She would have to meet him. Until she had spoken to him herself she would never know if he were the baby's father, or not.

'Did you know a Katharine Lang?' she asked Mrs Bundle suddenly. 'She came to London three years ago and I am fairly certain that she would have sought work here at the Lane.'

Mrs Bundle shook her head. 'Never bin 'ere,' she said firmly. 'I worked at this place these last fifteen years, and no Katharine Lang's ever bin 'ere, of that I'm certain.'

Grace sighed. Now that she was so busy with rehearsals she did not have any spare time, but once the play had begun she would have to visit other theatres in the mornings, to enquire about Kathy.

★ ★ ★

The night of the dress rehearsal everything went wrong, but Mrs Bundle declared that it was a good sign.

'You 'ave everythink going right at the dress rehearsal,' she said, 'and sure as anythink the Opening's a disaster.'

But this was little comfort to Grace who had been late for one entrance; her black gown in the Ballroom scene had been uncomfortably tight and had restricted both her voice and her breathing; and she felt that the other girls were laughing at her, delighting in her misfortune.

The invited audience had not appeared to notice these mishaps and had clapped long and hard at the end, but then Jemima Power and Lionel Chase were favourites with the London crowds, and had played opposite each other with deft humour.

'There, there,' said Mrs Bundle, as Grace sat dejectedly in front of a mirror, the last to get dressed and go home. 'Go on home wiv you and get some food into your stomach. It's bin a long day and everythink will be fine tomorrow.'

Grace wished suddenly that she was at home, back in Windhaven, and away from the smelly lamps, the hot atmosphere, and all the unfriendly girls.

She had received a curt little note from her father that week, thanking her for the money she had sent but declaring that he thought her behaviour both foolish and ungodly.

Her father was right. She should

44

never have agreed to becoming an actress; the theatre had been the cause of Kathy's misfortune and death, and it was making Grace, herself, miserable. But she would have to persevere for a while, until she had solved the problem of Sammy's future.

As she made her way out into the street, Grace saw Lord Jaspar Ede move forward into the lamplight.

'Allow me to escort you, Miss Fairweather. We must celebrate your success.'

'It was not a success and I am feeling very sorry for myself. Take me home, if you would be so kind, sir. I am weary and depressed.'

'That does not sound like you, Grace Fairweather,' chided Ede. 'Where is your courage?' He put his hand beneath her chin and tilted her face to meet his gaze. 'You did not do at all badly for your first public showing, and the few wrinkles will be ironed out at the final rehearsal tomorrow morning.'

'Oh, rehearsals — I'm sick to death

of them!' She pulled her head away from his grasp and began to walk down the street towards the Strand.

'Now, Miss Grace, you cannot go off in such ill humour.' Lord Jaspar hurried after her and caught hold of her arm, swinging her round to face him again. 'Come. My carriage is waiting and we'll partake of some food and wine and you will feel better in no time.'

Grace felt close to tears and went meekly to the coach with him. Perhaps food would be a good idea. There had been no time to return to her lodgings in between rehearsals, so she had taken a piece of bread and cheese to the theatre that morning. It had been eaten at noon, and now it was close to midnight. No wonder she was feeling cross and tired. Grace smiled a trifle wearily as her companion assisted her up into his carriage, and he thought that she appeared more beautiful than ever, more fragile and helpless than he had yet seen her.

If he was not careful, he decided, this

wench would be running off with his heart.

But Jaspar Ede was too wily a campaigner to be seduced by the looks of a female. Enjoy 'em, spoil 'em, love 'em, and leave 'em, was his motto. No woman was worth falling in love with; they were incapable of deep emotion and untrustworthy, to boot.

'Where are we?' Grace asked some while later, as her companion handed her out onto the pavement.

'I have brought you to my home in Bedford Square,' Ede answered, smiling down at her. 'I thought you would be too weary for noise and company, so we shall dine here in peaceful seclusion.'

A grave-faced butler opened the door to them, and Grace followed him down a long hallway to where a door was open on the right. She entered a spacious drawing-room, resplendent in gold and eau-de-Nil; chandeliers lit the room from above, and the carpet was of soft green and pink and yellow shades, deeper and thicker than anything she had trodden on before. There were several sofas covered in damask, and little embroidered footstools; dainty button-backed chairs, and a superb carved mantelpiece under which a fire was burning brightly.

Above the fireplace hung an oil painting of several naked females who appeared to be cavorting about in the sea. Grace turned her eyes quickly away from the picture. Her father would have been aghast at such an immodest painting in a gentleman's home.

'Do you not admire my Boucher?' asked his lordship, eyeing her confusion with some amusement. 'It is not as famous as his 'Diana', or the 'Triumph of Amphitrite', but I consider it a masterpiece, nonetheless.'

'It — it is not polite,' said Grace stiffly. Then she looked about her in admiration. 'But it is a lovely room otherwise.'

'My late mother's choice of furnishings,' remarked his lordship briefly. 'Somewhat old-fashioned now and I much prefer the more solid furniture and darker colours of the present. But,' he shrugged, 'I am too lazy to change it all at the moment.'

'I like it.'

The butler moved forward to take her shawl and gloves, and Grace stood, small and white-faced, in the lilac velvet gown which Ede had chosen for her. Her hair had been piled up on top of her head, and Mrs Bundle had threaded a lilac ribbon through the entwined tresses.

Lord Jaspar surveyed her with satisfaction.

'Now, we must get some colour into those cheeks of yours. Bring the wine here, Carlton,' he said to the butler, 'and we will come up to dine in half-an-hour.'

'Very good, sir.' The man bowed and withdrew.

'Come and sit down, Miss Grace, and rest yourself. The wine will help you to revive your spirits before we eat.'

She smiled across at him. He really

was the kindest man, and she was thankful that he had made her acquaintance and taken her under his wing, rather than the mysterious Lord P whom nobody liked.

Lord Jaspar seated himself beside her on the rose-coloured sofa which stood nearest to the fire, and placed a footstool beneath her feet.

'Now, lie back and tell me a little about yourself,' he said. 'I really know nothing about you although this must be our — what — fourth meeting?'

'Third,' said Grace, 'although I feel that I know *you* quite well.'

'Really?' His black brows lifted in amusement. 'And what do you know about me, Miss Grace?'

'That you are kind and generous, but do not think anything of it. That you are lonely, and, I do believe, a little bit sad.'

'My dear girl — ' he broke off as Carlton entered the room again bearing the wine.

As soon as she began to sip from that

first glass, Grace felt life returning to her and a sense of well-being began to seep through her tired limbs.

'Oh, that *is* good!' she exclaimed. 'If I had a great deal of money I would see that everyone in the village had a glass of wine to drink every day. It makes one feel better and more cheerful, and all one's problems melt away.'

'But you do not have problems, surely? You are too young to have experienced worries and woes.'

'They may not be big problems, but they are real, nonetheless,' she said.

'Tell me.' Lord Jaspar refilled her glass, which was now empty.

'Well,' said Grace, 'there are so many poor people in the village at home, we cannot help them all, although Father and I do our best, and it always seems to be the babies and young children who suffer most.'

'You like children?'

'Oh, yes!' said Grace. 'I hope to have a big family when I marry.'

'And have you a young man back in

the village?' asked his lordship. 'Who helps you with your charitable work, perhaps? Whom you admire?'

'No.' She dimpled. 'Though Farmer Laster's Tom is a kind lad.'

'Do you not enjoy his company?' Ede watched the girl closely.

'Sometimes,' Grace said, leaning her head back against the sofa and closing her eyes.

'Why only sometimes?' His lordship leaned closer to her and removed the glass from her hand. 'Is he not a handsome, well-made lad?'

Grace opened her eyes and saw Lord Jaspar's face very near her own; she admired his straight nose, and his thick black hair which sprang back from his proud forehead. His lips were firm, yet sensitive, and his eyes, appearing darker in the candle-light, caressed her own.

'Tom is not as handsome as you are, sir, and his hands — ' she paused, glancing down at his lordship's strong, beautifully-manicured fingers. Then she shuddered, closing her eyes again,

'Tom's hands are dirty, and his nails are broken and grimy,' she said.

'Have they touched you, Grace?' One hand lifted and his finger stroked her cheek, very lightly, almost a whisper of a caress. 'Have they stroked your skin, like this, sweetheart?'

Grace's eyes flew open and he saw her blush, from beneath the lilac velvet at her throat up to suffuse the whole of her face.

'Has he touched you, Grace?' Lord Jaspar insisted.

'No.' She sat forward abruptly, putting a hand to her head. 'Goodness me, I do feel strange. Shall we eat, sir? I do believe that I am the slightest bit tipsy.'

'We will eat when you have answered one more question. Have you ever been kissed?'

Her eyelids drooped, hiding the beauty of her grey eyes, and his lordship saw the faintest hint of that damned, enticing dimple.

'Only once, sir,' she answered demurely.

It had been a clumsy, sudden

embrace last Christmas, she remembered, and when it was over Grace had not been sure who was the most surprised by it, Tom Laster, or herself.

Lord Jaspar Ede looked at her mouth which was full and soft, slightly moist from the wine, and he longed to lean forward and taste her innocent lips. But not yet, he told himself, wait but a little longer. She must not be scared or affronted. She must come to him willingly, and she would, that very night! Of that he was certain.

★　★　★

When Grace awoke the next morning, she found herself lying in a large, soft bed. The room about her was high-ceilinged, and the curtains had been drawn apart so that bright rays of sunshine filtered in through the white lace drapes.

She sat up in fright staring around her, then slid hurriedly beneath the covers again as she realised that she was clad only in her chemise, and that her head ached abominably.

What had happened to her? And where was she?

Grace turned her head gingerly from side to side, taking in the sturdy, mirrored dressing-table, the carved wooden wardrobe against the wall, and the splendid marble wash-stand at the far end of the room. Then her horrified eyes lit upon a man's crumpled shirt, which had been thrown carelessly over the back of a chair by the window, and a pair of trousers which lay upon the floor near the fireplace. Her cheeks burned as she noticed a starched white collar upon the dresser top, lying next to a gold watch and chain.

This was a gentleman's bedchamber and she must now be lying in Lord Jaspar's own bed.

Desperately, she cast her mind back to the night before. What had happened after the meal? How had she come to be in this room? Why was she not at home with Joan and Samuel in Cecil Street?

But try as she would, Grace could remember nothing save for the delicious meal which had been served by the grave-faced butler. She had ascended to the first floor with his lordship, had sat opposite him at the polished table, and she could remember having admired the exquisite linen, the gleaming silver candlesticks, the crystal goblets, and the silver cutlery which had been engraved with his initials. She could also remember intense hunger and an overwhelming thirst, and wine, more and more wine.

Grace shivered and slid further down the bed. It was that treacherous liquid which had proved her undoing; that, and the very obvious charm of her companion. He had been so handsome sitting opposite her in the candlelight, so attentive and admiring that her silly head had been turned. She could remember laughing, far too much, and drinking in the same dreadful and uncontrolled manner.

And now here she was, lying in Lord Jaspar's bed. Who had undressed her? What had happened during those lost hours?

Suddenly, anger replaced fear, and Grace clenched her fists at her sides. How dared he use her thus! He, who was a man of the world, a titled gentleman, and an experienced older man, how dared he take advantage of her! Especially when he knew her to be fresh from the country and quite ignorant of the immoral and wicked ways of city folk.

As she lay fuming in silent wrath, the door of the bedchamber opened and his lordship entered.

'Ah, you are awake at last, I see.' Ede was dressed in a pale gold silk dressing-gown. His thick black hair looked decidedly unkempt, and his wide jaw was unshaven. 'I know that you are worked hard at the theatre, Miss Fairweather, but such sloth is not creditable. If you do not rouse yourself fairly speedily, you will be late for the final rehearsal.'

He walked over to the wardrobe and drew out her gown.

'Kindly clothe yourself, and I shall hold myself ready to assist with any fastenings. As to your hair, I regret that you must manage that yourself. Possessing no lady's maid, I cannot offer you her services, and I doubt that my valet has experience of such matters.'

Ede advanced upon the bed and gazed down at her rigid form with some amusement. 'Do not worry about my presence, dear girl, I put you to bed last night so have already perceived all that you are now trying so desperately to hide!' He laid her gown upon the end of the bed and held out his hand. 'Come, Miss Fairweather, arise like my Boucher nymphs and make your ablutions. You cannot lie there forever. I shall remove myself from your presence whilst you wash, unless, that is, you require my assistance?'

'Get out!' Grace's voice was thick

with emotion, and she had some difficulty in finding the words she needed. 'You are a despicable scoundrel, sir, and I am surprised that you dare to enter this room. Get out and leave me this instant!'

Ede's eyebrows rose and he looked down at her with faint surprise. 'Those are ungracious words for one who carried you to bed because you were unable to walk, and who gave you, moreover, the comfort and warmth of his own bed for your night's repose.'

'I hate you!' Grace struggled to a sitting position, clutching the bed covers to her heaving breast. 'I hate your house, and your hospitality, and your immoral ways!' Her red hair tumbled about her shoulders in wild confusion, and her brows were drawn down over her stormy grey eyes. Her face glowed with anger and she looked dishevelled, passionate, and infinitely desirable.

Lord Jaspar Ede stared down at her, cursing the extraordinary sense of chivalry which had stopped him from taking advantage of her. Why had he not taken her the night before, as he had longed to do? Why the devil had he not seduced her, instead of passing an uncomfortable night on the hard couch in his study next door?

He dragged his eyes away from the girl's voluptuous form and walked swiftly to the door. Then he stopped and looked back at her.

'If this display of temper is due to the fact that you believe you have lost your virginity,' he said curtly, 'then I would advise you to guard your shrewish tongue. I have not touched you except to remove your outer clothing, so your chastity is quite safe, miss.'

Grace stared back at his set face, and saw that his yellow-flecked eyes appeared to burn with an anger as great as her own.

'I may be a rogue and a rake, Miss Fairweather, but I can assure you that it would give me no pleasure to seduce an inert and intoxicated female. Once you have learnt to drink with restraint and dignity, you might appear more attractive to male eyes. But as it was, you appeared as enticing as a little pig, and snored as loudly as any porker. No, my dear, when I take my pleasure I desire both beauty and daintiness, and as you possessed neither quality last night, you were quite safe from my attentions.'

Lord Jaspar left the room, closing the door firmly behind him.

Grace clambered out of bed, still trembling with rage. What a rude and insufferable man he was! If she had had too much to drink, then it was entirely his fault.

She washed quickly, noticing with grim pleasure that a great deal of water had slopped over the side of the basin and was now darkening the carpet beneath the stand. She hoped that it would prove to be a permanent stain. Then she padded back to the bed and pulled on the gown over her head. Unfortunately, the fastenings were at the back and as she had not bothered with her lacing, she could not manage to bring the two sides of the bodice together at all.

Her face burning with frustration, she strode across to the fireplace and pulled the bell rope with all her might. She did not care *who* came in answer to her summons. It could be his lordship, or that sour-faced butler, or the cook, herself. All she required was instant assistance with her clothing, so that she was presentable enough for the street and could make her way home as speedily as possible. She was so angry that she cared not a fig for whom might appear in the doorway.

Grace gave another furious tug at the rope and at the same moment Jaspar Ede put his head round the door.

'You rang?' he queried.

'Yes.' She was only just able to control the curses which lay upon the tip of her tongue, coarse words which she had never uttered before but which she had often heard in the dressing-room at the Lane, and which would have applied very nicely to the black-haired brute who now moved forward in a leisurely fashion to confront her.

'Do up my gown so that I may leave here at the earliest possible moment,' Grace snapped.

'Say please.' His lordship's anger seemed to have cooled, and he advanced slowly, eyeing her flushed face and ruffled appearance with an infuriating look of interest on his lean face.

'Please.' She spat out the word, her bosom heaving with passion.

'If you will swell up like a turkey cock I have no hope of bringing these two edges together,' announced Lord Jaspar, his hands warm on her back, and his breath fanning her naked shoulders.

Clasping her hands before her and squeezing her eyes tightly shut, Grace endeavoured to control both her temper and her breathing.

'That is better.' His hands tugged at the velvet bodice none too gently and then, with a grunt of satisfaction, Ede brought the first hook and eye together and began fastening the rest.

'You are not as slender as I had imagined,' he remarked, spinning her round by the shoulders, his eyes moving appreciatively over her body. 'Your dresser must have one devil of a job lacing you for that black taffeta in the Ballroom scene.' He stepped back, still gazing at her with impolite curiosity. 'But I never did care for skinny females and find rounded curves far more enticing.'

If he had been two steps closer Grace would have slapped his face. As it was, she walked away from him to the dressing-table and began fumbling with her tangled mane of hair. The lilac ribbon had disappeared and without a brush, or her little bowl of pins, she was incapable of doing anything with such confusion. Fuming silently, she bent and pulled open the top drawer of the dresser before her, where she found a neat pile of silk handkerchiefs. Grace lifted one out, gave it a swift flick, then folded it into a triangle and placed it over her hair, tying it beneath her chin in a firm knot.

'There, that will have to do. Where is my shawl? And kindly give orders for your carriage. I must leave at once.'

Lifting her head, she gazed imperiously at her companion. Never would she speak to him again. He was impossibly arrogant and must have a most dreadful reputation. How could Mrs Bundle have believed him to be a perfect gentleman? He obviously knew everything there was to know about females — the unspeakable kind, that was — and had had every intention of seducing her the night before, of that she was certain. Fortunately for her, she had consumed too much wine and had passed out before his lordship could have his way with her. But it was all over now, she never intended seeing him again, and it was best if she forgot all about that dreadful night as quickly as possible.

The butler held out her shawl in an

imperturbable manner, as if young girls spent the night with his master every week and came downstairs with ker-chiefs over their hair as a matter of course. Lord Jaspar opened the door for her with an obsequious bow. Grace tossed her head in the air and walked past him without a glance. To her great relief the carriage stood waiting in the street outside. Aware of how ridiculous she must appear in her velvet gown and cashmere shawl, topped by a man's white silk handkerchief, Grace climbed swiftly into the carriage and was driven away.

★ ★ ★

'Where was you all night? I was that worried about you.' Joan stared accus-ingly at her, as Grace entered the sitting-room and threw off her shawl with a little sigh of relief.

It was none of the nurse's business and Grace disliked the tone of her voice, but Joan was obviously anxious and as she relied upon Grace for her living, it was natural that she should be upset by her non-appearance.

'I was very tired after the Dress Rehearsal, and Lord Ede asked me to dine with him,' said Grace, removing the kerchief from her head. 'Unfortunately I drank rather too much wine and Lord Ede's housekeeper put me to bed and allowed me to remain in her room until this morning.'

It was a small lie but a necessary one. Grace did not care for the knowing expression on Joan's pale face, and could not have her telling tales when they eventually returned to the village.

'How is Sammy?' she went on quickly. 'I'll just have a quick look at him and then I must go to the theatre.'

'Don't you wake him, miss — just got him to sleep, I have.'

Grace tiptoed over to the cradle and gazed down at the slumbering child.

'Don't know what your pa's going to say about all these comings and goings, and him being a clergyman, and all.'

Joan's voice sounded behind her, surly and objectionable. 'He won't like the way you're carrying on, Miss Grace, that's for sure.'

Grace straightened and stepped back from the cradle. 'Perhaps you would like to return to Windhaven now, Joan?' she suggested.

The girl had grumbled incessantly about being left on her own so much, and about missing her friends and family.

'I'll go gladly, miss. But I'll be taking Sammy with me.'

'Sammy remains here,' said Grace. 'I must find his father and give him a chance in life. I promised Kathy I'd see to that.'

'You'll never find his father!' Joan snorted, pushing at her lank brown hair which she refused to tie back off her shoulders. 'And how can you look after Sammy without me? You've no milk, and you're at that theatre place all day and most of the night.'

Grace hesitated. She knew that there

were old women who took in babies and young children whilst the mothers worked, she had heard tales about them from the other girls at the Lane. But the stories had been gruesome and mainly about deaths from dirty feeding habits, and appalling living conditions. No, she could not manage without Joan, not until she had found Lord P. Then, if he were wealthy enough, and truly Samuel's father, then Joan could be dismissed and another, respectable wet-nurse engaged for the little boy.

Grace sighed and pushed past Joan to go to her own room.

'Be patient just a little longer, if you please. I am doing my best for Sammy and it is him we ought to be thinking about. Give me a few more weeks and if I haven't met Lord P by then, I promise that you and the baby can return to Windhaven and I shall follow the moment the play ends its run.'

'Then I need more money.' Joan's small eyes watched Grace's face. 'A shilling a week is not enough for my needs and by Sunday I've nothing left to spend.'

Sunday was Joan's day off and Grace loved these days, for then she cared for the baby on her own and made believe that he was her son. Joan returned at midday to feed him, and to get food for herself, but she was out of the rooms all morning and afternoon, and it was the day Grace loved best; no theatre, she could wear her old and most comfortable gown, and she pottered about, singing and sewing, and spending a great deal of time cuddling Sammy.

She turned now and looked at Joan. If she gave her more money there would be less to send home to Father. But she needed Joan. For the moment she would have to give in to blackmail.

'Very well,' Grace said curtly. 'As from Friday I shall give you two shillings a week, but that will be the limit so do not come begging for more in a few weeks' time.'

'In a few weeks I shan't be here,' answered Joan tartly. 'Me and Sammy will be back where we belong — you said so!'

'I said *you* would be. By then, Sammy will be with his rightful father.'

Never would she allow Sammy to go back to Joan's family. Grace had seen the place but once, when she went to engage the girl's services before coming to London, and she had been shocked by what she had seen.

Joan's father and her two older brothers were farm labourers so money came into the dwelling each week. But the Crump home, if such a comfortable sounding word could be applied to it, was a filthy shack at the very end of the village. The roof had half-collapsed, letting in rain on every wet day, and the floor had been a mess of damp clay on the day that Grace had visited. Three young children had fought and tumbled about in the slime, whilst a grey-faced woman had suckled an infant to her withered breast.

All the family slept huddled together at the back of the room, and it was not known whether Joan's dead baby had been sired by one of her brothers, or by her own father.

Grace had come away from the place filled with revulsion but she had felt compassion for the sallow-faced girl, and was glad to offer her a chance to get away from her family.

Remembering all this now, Grace was determined that Sammy would never return to live amongst the Crumps. She also wondered at Joan's impertinence in criticising her life in London. The girl's own life had been far from innocent. And she should have been grateful for what Grace was doing for her; the lodgings with Mrs Luce were infinitely cleaner and more comfortable than the squalor she had left behind in Windhaven, and Grace was paying her the first money she had ever earned in her life.

4

The Opening Night, as Mrs Bundle had predicted, was a great success. The audience was enthusiastic and laughed in all the right places; Grace remembered her words and grew in confidence as the scenes passed; and there were ten curtain calls at the end of the evening, with the audience on its feet, clamoring for the author.

Crispin Mellish, his collar askew and his face red and shiny with exhilaration, kissed all the girls when the curtain fell for the last time and thanked everyone for making his *Countess* a success.

When Grace returned to her dressing-room she felt elated. It had been a wonderful experience and she knew that in a small way she had contributed to the perfection of the evening.

'You looked a real picture, lovey,' said Mrs Bundle, helping her to disrobe.

And for once the other girls, and even sour-faced Violet Hill, were smiling and joking with her, all animosity forgotten for the moment.

As they were removing their grease-paint, chattering and jostling before the inadequate mirrors, there was a knock at the door.

'Now who can that be?' Mrs Bundle trotted over to the door. 'Some admirer, I've no doubt, wot's slipped past old Ben.'

Visitors were not encouraged back-stage, at least not gentlemen callers who desired to see one of the bit players. The principal performers could invite friends and relations into their dressing-rooms, but the management made firm rules about gentlemen calling for the girls. They had to remain in the alley outside the stage door and greet the girls only when they went out into the street. But if the gentleman was wealthy a large tip would be enough to close old Ben's eyes long enough to allow a hurried entrance to the building.

There was a murmur of voices outside in the corridor, and all heads turned to look at Mrs Bundle's broad back which filled the half-open doorway. Who was calling? And who was the lucky girl who had been singled out for attention?

'Grace!' Mrs Bundle called over her shoulder, and once again Grace was aware of sidelong jealous glances, and the whisper of envious tongues, as she pulled her wrapper closer around her body and went to join the dresser in the doorway. If it were Lord Jaspar she would slam the door in his face!

But it was not his lordship. As Mrs Bundle stepped back, tactfully closing the door behind her, Grace looked up into the most beautiful face she had ever seen.

It was a man's face, and he stood, not very tall, a few inches higher than Grace herself, clutching a bouquet of deep red roses.

'I am Richard Mercury,' he said, in a light, musical voice, and he smiled and held out the flowers to her.

Astonished, Grace took the blooms, her eyes never leaving the stranger's face.

He had golden hair, very shiny, curling on his wide forehead and growing somewhat longer at the back so that the curls rested on his winged collar. Mr Mercury's skin was clear, and there was a faint flush on his cheeks. His mouth was generous and well-formed, and when he smiled she saw perfect, strong white teeth. Deep blue eyes stared back at her in the flickering lamplight, fringed by long, dark blond lashes. Mr Mercury wore a long coat of dark blue cloth, with a velvet collar and two bright shiny buttons at his neat waist.

He had the face of an angel, Grace thought incredulously, no man had the right to be so beautiful. Who was this Mr Richard Mercury? And why had he brought flowers for her?

The stranger answered her unspoken questions.

'I have come with a message, Miss Fairweather,' he said, in his soft voice, very pleasing to the ear. 'Lord Pridmont sends these roses and wishes me to say how enchanted he was by your performance tonight. He greatly desires your presence at dinner, if you are not too weary for company?'

Grace tried to collect her scattered wits. She was tired and had intended going straight home after the performance. But here, at last, was the chance to meet Lord Pridmont and to find out if he had known Kathy. She could not turn down this opportunity, but she was wary. After one night of fear and confusion, she was not going to be caught out again.

'I do not go out without a chaperon,' she answered slowly, 'and my maid is not with me tonight.'

Richard Mercury bowed. 'I shall be in attendance for the entire evening, Miss Fairweather, and will make it my duty to escort you safely back to your lodgings once the meal is over.'

Mrs Bundle was not pleased to hear Grace's news and when Violet and the other girls had left the dressing-room, she told Grace so.

'That man 'as caused more distress and unhappiness than anyone else I've 'eard tell of,' she said grumpily, brushing out Grace's long red hair and then plaiting it into a thick, shining rope of burnished bronze.

'Have you ever met him?' Grace adjusted the black taffeta frills at her bosom, hoping that the gown would be suitable for Lord Pridmont's dinner invitation.

Mrs Bundle had suggested that she wore it, for her chintz, which she had worn to the theatre that day, was not suitable for evening attire and she did not want to keep Richard Mercury waiting by going all the way home to change. Cleaning her face of grease-paint and re-arranging her hair was taking long enough as it was.

'Never met Lord P.' Mrs Bundle wound the long plait around Grace's small head so that it gave her a regal air and looked like a coronet. 'Seen 'im, I 'ave, in that box on the left. Always there on a first night, 'e is. Takin' 'is pick, choosing silly young girls like you, Miss Grace, for 'is pleasure.'

'What did you call him?' Grace was staring at the dresser's reflection in the mirror.

'Lord P. Always known 'im as that, nasty old man.'

'That was what Kathy said, only I thought she was trying to say his full name. Are you *sure* you didn't know Kathy Lang?'

'Told you, lovey, never did 'ear that name. But I remember one girl wot called 'im Lord P. Went out wiv 'im a lot, she did.' Mrs Bundle put one hand to her brow, frowning in concentration. 'Dearie me, now wot was 'er name? I'll get it in a minute.'

'Never mind that now,' said Grace impatiently, 'please finish my hair and you can tell me tomorrow if you remember. I have kept that nice Mr

Mercury waiting long enough, as it is.'

'Nice Mr Mercury, indeed! Tarred wiv the same brush, if you ask me. Now don't you go trusting neither of them gentlemen, Miss Grace, and I warns you, don't come crying to me when it's too late.'

'I have only one intention and that is of finding Kathy's Lord P and asking him to be responsible for little Sammy's future. After that, I shall be glad when this run is over and I can return to the country. At least one knows who one's real friends are there.'

Grace thought a trifle wistfully about Tom Laster. He was honest and trustworthy, a really good young man, and Grace knew that she would have been safe in his company.

There might have been a lack of splendour and luxury in the village of Windhaven, but security and tranquillity were rather special qualities, Grace realised suddenly, and seemingly rare in the city of London. Maybe Kathy would have fared better if she had settled for a country lad like Tom, instead of seeking the excitement and novelty of the unreal theatre-land.

Giving her head a little shake and smiling a farewell at the dresser, Grace wrapped her shawl about her shoulders and went downstairs to find Richard Mercury waiting patiently beside a carriage in the street outside.

On the way to Cavendish Square, Mercury complimented Grace once more upon her performance, and said how much Lord Pridmont had enjoyed the play.

'Do not, I pray, be put off by his lordship's somewhat unfortunate appearance,' he added, as the carriage rattled on its way. 'Lord Pridmont is a great romantic and loves all the beauty and magic of fairy tales. He has been blessed with neither good looks nor good health himself, but is a very wealthy man and thus manages to forget much that would otherwise have troubled him.'

Grace looked curiously at her companion. What a strange speech!

'For how long have you known Lord Pridmont?' she asked. 'Do you live with him? Are you employed by him?'

The young man smiled, and Grace felt her heart lurch at the beauty of his face.

'Everything I am, and all that I possess, is due to his lordship,' Mercury replied. 'He found me as a starving waif in the gutters of Fetter Street, aged — we know not what — perhaps three, or four years old? And he took me in, clothed, fed and educated me, and he will have my gratitude until the day I die.'

He spoke with great fervour and Grace wished that Mrs Bundle could have heard his words. Here, at least, was one person who spoke well of the mysterious Lord P.

'Has he a wife?' she queried.

'No.' Richard Mercury shot her a look from his corner of the carriage. 'I believe he would like to marry, but his wife must be a very special lady. Lord Pridmont is most particular, and although he is a great admirer of feminine beauty, he desires much more than mere good looks from any future bride.'

Had he known Kathy? Grace gazed out of the window and pondered. Her friend had been a beautiful girl, with a pleasant nature and a gay sense of humour in the old days. But she had been lowly born and doubtless not of high enough rank to become the bride of a peer. But if Lord Pridmont were indeed Sammy's father, surely he would have made some settlement upon the girl and her son? Did he know that Kathy had produced a child? Maybe she had hidden herself away in shame when she knew she was to have a baby? And only returned to Windhaven when she realised she was mortally sick? But then again, maybe Lord Pridmont was *not* Sammy's father and her search would have to begin all over again on the morrow?

Dearie me, thought Grace, there were so many questions to be answered, would the truth ever be discovered? Or would she have to return to the village in a month, or so, knowing as little as she did now?

At that moment the carriage drew to a halt before a gracious white mansion of some considerable size, and when Richard Mercury assisted her down to the pavement, Grace saw that a footman stood in the lighted doorway above her, resplendent in silk stockings, black breeches, scarlet jacket and powdered wig. Thankful that she had worn the black taffeta gown, she placed her hand on Mr Mercury's arm and allowed him to lead her up the steps.

Inside she found herself in a wide hall where marble columns supported a frescoed ceiling; chandeliers hung in glistening clusters above her head, and numerous Persian rugs lay upon the polished boards at her feet. A red carpet covered the staircase which led to the floor above, and on the walls hung oil paintings which portrayed naked females, similar to the one in Lord

Ede's drawing-room. Grace averted her eyes and looked instead at the marble-topped tables which stood about the hall, supporting Chinese vases and delicate porcelain figurines. It was all very luxurious and magnificent, and rather overwhelming to the girl from a country vicarage. She had admired Lord Ede's establishment, but this house was many times more splendid in both proportion and content.

'Come with me, Miss Grace.' Mercury led her up the stairs to the landing where passages led off to left and right. 'We will find his lordship in his favourite room,' announced her companion. 'You will be surprised by it but also, I think, delighted. Come and see.'

He walked down the passage on their left to a white door which sported a golden knob. Another footman stood outside and on seeing them he bowed and took Grace's shawl and Mercury's coat, before opening the door for them.

Faint sounds of music came to Grace's ears but she was scarcely aware of the noise, all her senses were concentrated upon what she saw before her. In the middle of the large room, reclining on a heap of satin and velvet cushions, lay a very fat man. He was dressed in loose fitting robes, all white, and a white turban was upon his head. The only colour was in the cushions, a dazzling mound of scarlets and emerald greens, deep sapphires and bright yellows. She saw, incredulously, that his feet were bare, and that on his small plump hands were many rings, set with the same coloured gems as the cushions on which he lay; emeralds, rubies and sapphires.

'Welcome, my dear Miss Fairweather.' Lord Pridmont possessed a thick, deep voice, and his face was unhealthily pale, as white as the turban upon his head. Two tiny black eyes peeped out at her from between mounds of doughlike flesh, and his mouth was a little pink rosebud above double chins. He did not appear to have eyebrows, in fact his skin was totally hairless.

Grace swallowed, trying to hide her repugnance at such a figure, and moved forward to curtsey.

'I hope you can make yourself comfortable on the floor — cannot abide wooden furniture and stiff upright posture. Give her plenty of cushions, Rich, it will take a little time for our young lady to accustom herself to our informality.'

All the time he was speaking, Grace could feel him watching her with his intent, currant-like eyes.

Mercury brought forward several cushions from a pile beneath one of the tall pot-plants, and Grace sprawled awkwardly, crushing her gown beneath her and feeling extremely foolish. There was no furniture in the large room, apart from a painted screen at the far end, but a great many pots and tubs, filled with palms and other green-leaved plants, occupied spaces all over the floor. The atmosphere was warm and humid, and the strange reed-like music, which whispered through the air, added to the feeling of unreality.

'My musicians are behind the screen,' grunted his lordship. 'Cannot bear the sight of them but like the sounds they make. Now, we must eat. You must be hungry after that excellent performance. Forgive me for not staying to congratulate you, but I find the seating at that theatre so uncomfortable I cannot wait to return to my place here. Knew Rich would deliver you to me in good time.' Lord Pridmont's mouth disappeared completely between folds of bulging skin and Grace realised that he was smiling.

He then clapped his soft hands with a little puff of sound and the footman, who must have had very keen hearing, opened the door from outside and came immediately into the room.

'Bring food — at once!' ordered Pridmont.

The footman bowed and withdrew.

'Tell me about yourself,' said his lordship, gazing once more at Grace and lolling back upon his cushions.

Mercury had seated himself, cross-legged, on a mat between Lord Pridmont and herself, and he looked perfectly at ease in such a position. But Grace felt undignified and at a disadvantage, not knowing whether to sit up straight, or half-lie, like his lordship. Supporting herself on one hand, and trying to appear as relaxed as possible, Grace told Lord Pridmont her story. To her disappointment his expression did not change when she mentioned Kathy, and she felt certain that he had not heard the girl's name before.

'So, you are seeking the lover of this Katharine Lang,' murmured his lordship, his fat little fingers stroking one of his chins. 'I fear that you are looking for a needle in a haystack, my dear Miss Fairweather. Have you no knowledge of his whereabouts? No hint of a clue as to whom he was?'

'Only that Kathy said he was a lord, and that his name began with the letter P.' She felt her heart begin to thud beneath her tightly-laced bodice. Had she gone too far? Would her host be angered by her words?

To Grace's relief, his face squeezed itself into that same grimace and his mouth disappeared between folds of skin. Lord Pridmont smiled.

'If I were, indeed, the father of this poor abandoned Samuel, I should naturally do right by the child and provide for his future. But we have not known a Miss Katharine Lang, have we, Rich?'

The young man turned his brilliant eyes upon the older man and shook his head. 'I am certain that we do not know the young lady, sir.'

'Perhaps you are aware that I admire feminine beauty, Miss Fairweather?' Pridmont looked across at her. 'Being old and ugly myself, I am constantly searching for consolation and find both tranquillity of mind, and delight, in beautiful objects. You, dear Miss Fairweather, are to my sad eyes as perfect as a spring meadow — so natural and unspoilt. When I look in the mirror the sight fills me with despair, but what I see before me now gladdens my heart and gives me hope.'

Grace felt her cheeks burn with embarrassment and she lowered her head in confusion. After her strict, almost puritanical upbringing she found compliments difficult to accept in a composed manner.

'She is quite lovely, is she not, Rich?'

'Indeed, sir. So gentle and humble a maid is a rarity in London, and we are privileged to know her.'

'Nonsense!' Grace cried out, recovering herself with a jolt and finding these speeches too flowery for her liking. 'I assure you that I am quite ordinary, and refuse to have my head turned by your extravagant phrases!'

'Well said, young lady,' Pridmont chuckled. 'I can see that vanity is not one of your faults. Now, here comes our little repast, I hope you will find some of the dishes to your taste.'

Two footmen marched forward

bringing with them two little low tables which they placed in front of Richard Mercury. Then numerous small bowls were set upon the tables, accompanied by snowy napkins and silver spoons.

'I do not drink alcohol,' said Lord Pridmont, 'I like to keep my mind clear and my senses acute. But we will have coffee after the meal.'

Grace heaved a sigh of relief. After the drama of the night before, she never wished to taste wine again. But she could not help marvelling at the strangeness of life. Here she was, Grace Fairweather from the village of Windhaven, dining two nights in a row with different peers of the realm!

'You smile, Miss Fairweather. May I ask what amuses you?'

The servants had departed and Richard Mercury was sitting forward, helping himself to various containers, piling the contents into an empty bowl in his hands.

Grace lifted her free hand in a little gesture of apology. 'Forgive me, sir, I did not mean to be rude, but it suddenly struck me that here I was, a simple girl from the country and quite unused to splendour, dining in the presence of a lord!'

'Perhaps there will be even more to wonder at in the days to come.' Pridmont straightened his slumped body and Mercury put down his bowl and stood up. Then he moved across to his companion and rearranged the cushions at his back, helping him to a more comfortable position. Then he held out one of the napkins, which Pridmont tucked beneath his fat chins.

'What have you chosen for me, Rich?'

'A little venison, some slices of veal, rice and baby carrots, sir.'

His lordship grunted, took the spoon which Mercury held out to him, and then accepted the bowl which the young man had already filled. Then he held the china close beneath his chin and began shovelling the contents into his mouth, at great speed and rather noisily.

'Please help yourself, Miss Grace.' Mercury gestured at the tables before them. 'Try something from several dishes. They mix well and I believe you will find them interesting. We have a cook who excels at exotic and unusual sauces.'

Grace was unable to identify any of the food set out before her, but the smell was appetising so she helped herself and then sat back stretching out her legs before her. She wished that she had some support for her back which was beginning to ache; it really was a most uncomfortable way to dine.

However, the food was delicious, small pieces of meat enveloped in rich gravies, with rice, and several vegetables cut up in buttered sauces. It was unusual fare, and the absence of knives and forks was somewhat disconcerting, but, avoiding the sight of his lordship, she followed Richard Mercury's actions and held the bowl close to her body and used the spoon to carry the food to her mouth.

'I have formed a liking for you, Miss Fairweather,' announced Lord Pridmont between mouthfuls, 'and Rich and I will do our best to help you in your quest for Samuel's father. Won't we, Rich?'

'Of course, sir.'

Grace was thankful to see that the young man was neat and careful in his habits, displaying none of his lordship's disgusting heartiness.

'You must visit us again, my dear young lady, and if you have had no success we will think of some way to assist you.'

'Thank you, sir.' She looked hastily away as a dribble of sauce ran down the man's chin and disappeared beneath the folds of his napkin.

'I shall give you one week, young lady, and then you must come here and dine, and inform us of any progress. Are your lodgings quite comfortable?' He changed the subject abruptly. 'Are they clean?'

'Yes, thank you, sir.'

'And you have a maid with you, so Rich informed me. Quite right. No young girl should live on her own — very risky. I am sure your father must worry about you. Have you any other relatives besides?'

'No, only Father. And I have promised him to return home the moment this play finishes. He is not happy at my staying so long in London.' She dimpled. 'But I manage to send money back to him each week, so he is grateful for that.'

'Of course,' murmured Pridmont, wiping his mouth and removing the napkin from around his neck, 'money is so important. We cannot exist without it.'

'But it is not for him,' Grace put in quickly. 'Father could manage on next to nothing, his wants are few. But he tries to help the poor in the parish and they, alas, are many.'

'What a virtuous creature you are, to be sure.' Pridmont stared across at her. 'Sending money home when you could be spending it on yourself. How did you manage to buy that gown, Miss Fairweather? Have you found yourself a wealthy protector, by any chance?'

Grace blushed deeply as she saw both Pridmont's and Mercury's eyes upon her. His lordship was frowning, as if displeased about something, but Mercury's gaze was warm, and filled with admiration.

'This gown, if you will hear the truth, is the one I wear in the Ballroom Scene. I am ashamed to admit that I borrowed it for this evening, having nothing else suitable to wear.'

As both men laughed, Grace relaxed and sat forward, placing her empty bowl beside her. 'I must also admit that Lord Jaspar Ede took me shopping soon after I arrived in London. But he told me that he would charge the bill to the theatre. I certainly would not want to be beholden to him for anything.'

'Why?' asked Pridmont sharply. 'Do you not like the man?'

'He is a rascal,' said Grace heatedly.

'Has he caused you alarm, my dear? Tell me if he has done aught to frighten or hurt you? We have never been friends, and there is a score or two which I would dearly like to settle with Jaspar Ede.'

Grace stared at the man opposite her, and, unbidden, the face and figure of Lord Jaspar came into her mind. That handsome, dark face, the disturbing tawny eyes; his charm, his generosity, and his sudden, devastating smile which transformed his lean and serious face.

'He is arrogant,' she said softly.

But she remembered his kindness when they first met, and the way in which he had spent time and money on her, helping to choose the clothes which best suited her, and sending her to Miss Kelly for all those lessons. He had not actually harmed her; he had simply acted in a high-handed and domineering manner.

'What has Lord Jaspar done to invoke your anger, Miss Grace?' Mercury spoke gently, his voice warming her with its tone.

'He has not done anything to me, sir.' Grace smiled at the young man. 'But I dislike his behaviour and sarcastic tongue and have vowed never to speak to him again. Do not worry about me, I beg. I have learnt my lesson and shall accept no more favours from him, that is certain.'

'No doubt he tried to seduce you.' Mercury rose lightly to his feet and walked over to the door, as Grace hung her head in confusion. 'Ede is a most arrogant and dangerous rake, and you are right to ignore him in the future. But I shall watch over you, Miss Grace, and be your guardian angel.' He flashed a smile at her and then spoke to the footman at the door.

How strange that he should use that word, thought Grace, watching him as he moved back to seat himself on the floor opposite her. He was, indeed, as fair and perfect as an angel, making Lord Jaspar, in comparison, seem very black and sardonic. She did not contemplate Lord Pridmont; he was so unattractive that she avoided looking at him as much as possible.

The footmen came again, bearing away the bowls and empty dishes, laying in their stead a silver pot of coffee and a matching cream jug and sugar bowl. The china cups were tiny and delicately fluted, and there were also plates of biscuits, wafer-thin, and marzipan fruits, and chocolate bon-bons. Lord Pridmont devoured many of these sweet-meats, and drank numerous cups of coffee, ladling both cream and sugar into his cup so that Grace was not surprised by his obesity. Richard Mercury, she was glad to see, nibbled at one biscuit and drank his coffee black, as she did.

Later that night as Mercury escorted her home in Lord Pridmont's carriage, Grace was very aware of him sitting beside her on the padded seat. She wondered what she would do if he tried to kiss her. She knew that it was too early in their acquaintanceship to allow such a liberty, yet she rather hoped that he might try. She found Richard Mercury very attractive. As well as being the most beautiful person she had ever seen, he was less frightening than Lord Jaspar, being small-boned and delicate of movement; he was also considerably cleaner, and more intelligent than Tom Laster.

As Grace pondered, a small smile dimpling her cheek, Mercury stretched out his hand and took hers in his grasp.

'You are a lovely and rather special girl, Miss Grace, and both Lord Pridmont and I wish to see more of you,' he said. 'I shall be waiting in the carriage outside the theatre every evening from now on, so if there is any trouble with Ede do not hesitate to come to me. But if all goes well I shall not expect you until one week from today. Do you understand?'

Grace nodded, looking across at his half-shadowed face in the corner beside her, feeling her heart beat faster at the touch of his fingers, and at the admiring gleam which she could just make out in his thickly-fringed eyes.

'Then I shall collect you to dine with us again. Have you an evening gown besides that taffeta, by the way? Or would you accept a small sum to buy yourself a new gown? You must dress up for Lord Pridmont,' he explained hastily, 'and several other dresses will be necessary.'

'I already have two other gowns for evening,' replied Grace a trifle haughtily, removing her hand from Mercury's, and straightening with a jerk. 'Would his lordship prefer white brocade, or yellow organdie?'

'Now, Miss Grace, you are angry with me and that will not do!' There was wry amusement in her companion's voice, and he shifted his position and moved closer to her, reclaiming her hand.

'I do not like being treated like a child,' said Grace, 'and I saw exactly how his lordship lives, and realise that he likes to surround himself with beautiful and pleasing sights. I shall not disappoint him, Mr Mercury, be assured of that.'

'Then white brocade, if you please, ma'am,' answered the young man in mock humility, 'and I shall send an orchid for your bosom. Although I fear that you will outshine any bloom or jewel I care to send.' He lifted her fingers to his lips, and she felt his mouth, warm and dry, caress the back of her hand. Grace shivered, very aware of his closeness in the dark confines of the carriage interior. 'You enchant me, dearest girl, perhaps it is just as well that our journey ends here.'

The horses were pulled up as he spoke, and Mercury let go of her hand and bent away to open the door on his side of the carriage. Grace felt strangely depressed, wishing that she could have travelled further with him. She was rapidly losing her heart to the golden young man.

5

The following afternoon as Grace left her lodgings and made her way towards the Strand, she was suddenly aware of a figure at her side. Turning her head, she looked up at the lean countenance of Lord Jaspar Ede.

'I do not wish to speak to you,' she said, hurrying her steps, 'kindly leave me in peace, sir.'

'This is a free land and this street is a public thoroughfare, I believe. As we appear to be going in the same direction I shall continue on my way, Miss Fairweather.'

Infuriating man! Grace raised her chin and stared straight before her as they pounded the pavement in unison.

Lord Jaspar gazed down at her erect little figure, very neatly attired in dove grey chintz, and noticed the stubborn set to her chin. What a spitfire she was, to be sure. But so damned enticing! Somehow he must get on the right side of her and regain her friendship which he had so enjoyed until he made the wrong move that night at his home.

'I rather hoped that you might agree to dine with me again, Miss Fairweather, so that I can make amends for your last visit and prove how well-mannered and polite I can be on certain occasions.'

Grace gave her bonnet a decided twitch of annoyance and walked even faster. It was the wide-brimmed bonnet of grey velvet, topped by a bow of striped silver ribbon, and his lordship congratulated himself on his choice for her. She really looked very well indeed.

'You will not accept my invitation? Well, perhaps I was being presumptuous. But I also wish to say a few words to you, young lady, and they are words of warning, so you had best heed them.'

Grace could feel his eyes upon her, but she ignored both his look and words of appeal. Nothing which Lord

Jaspar said was of any interest to her.

'I wish to warn you against seeing Pridmont,' went on his lordship in a stoic manner, determined to have his say. 'You are unused to city ways and do not recognise vice and depravity. Pridmont and his young servant boy are both steeped in wickedness, and I would put you on your guard against them. You are innocent and vulnerable and I should hate to see you hurt by them.'

Grace stopped in her tracks and turned on her companion, stamping her neatly-shod foot in fury. 'How dare you! How dare you refer to Mr Mercury as a servant boy, he is nothing of the kind! And they have both shown me kindness and politeness. As for vice, sir, I wonder that you dare to utter such a word. I have never been so shamed as I was in your house, and would *never* accept advice from you. Lord Pridmont treated me with utmost respect, and Mr Mercury is a most genuine and charming young man. I may add that they have warned me against *you*, sir. I will now heed their warning and say goodbye. I never wish to see you, or speak to you, again.'

'So that is how the land lies,' murmured his lordship, clasping his hands behind his back and frowning thoughtfully down at her. 'Then you are indeed in trouble, my dear, and will rue the day you ever set eyes on that pair of devils.'

Grace turned with a toss of her head and saw the Lane before her. She scurried towards the theatre and did not glance in Lord Jaspar's direction as he raised his hat and bowed to her. She ran up the short flight of steps to the stage door and was quickly past Ben and then climbing the stairs to her dressing-room.

'Just look at them flowers!' Mrs Bundle greeted her, as she flung open the door. 'Arrived a few minutes ago. Roses and lilies and I don't know *wot*! You're a lucky girl, Miss Grace, if they're from that nice Lord Jaspar. But if not — ' she paused and sniffed, 'then you'd best be careful, young lady.'

'Oh, gloom and doom!' cried out Grace, flinging off her bonnet and shawl and hanging them on a peg. She liked to be the first to arrive each day, so that she could take her pick of the mirrors and get her face and hair done before the others came jostling and pushing for space. 'I was just beginning to enjoy myself in London and to meet interesting people, and now everyone keeps shaking their heads and pursing their lips and warning me of dire misfortune.'

Grace reached for the card which was tucked into the sweet-smelling bouquet, and her cheeks became pink as she read the note. 'They are from Mr Mercury,' she said, tilting her chin at the old dresser, 'not from your wretched Lord P. Please put them into water, Mrs Bundle, and I'll take them home with me tonight. Joan will enjoy seeing them in our rooms. They will pretty the place up and remind her of the countryside.'

'I don't know about Mr Mercury,' said the old woman sharply, 'but I do knows about Lord Pridmont, an' you're not going to like this, Miss Grace, but I'll be telling you all the same.'

'What now?' Grace stepped out of her dress and hung it up, before pulling on her wrapper and going to sit before one of the mirrors. 'Go on, tell me the worst.' She placed a muslin cloth over her hair and began to smear greasepaint on her face.

Mrs Bundle stumped across the room and put the flowers in a bowl of water on the window sill. Then she came up behind Grace and stood there, her hands on her hips.

'I've remembered the name of the girl wot got friendly wiv Lord P and I reckon she's your friend, all right.'

Grace stared at the woman's reflection in the glass. 'What makes you so sure? What was her name?'

'Kaye Fair, she was, and looking like you said wiv black curly hair and a pretty smile. She took 'er name part from you, the Fair bit, and Kaye bein' short for Katharine, like.'

'Kaye Fair,' muttered Grace, her hands dropping to her lap. 'I do believe that might have been Kathy. When was she here, Mrs Bundle? Are the dates right?'

'Don't know about that but she must 'ave come to the Lane, wot — two, maybe three years ago? An' all the time she were 'ere that Lord Pridmont made a nuisance of 'imself wiv 'er. And she were so scatterbrained and foolish — 'A real live lord, Bundle!' — she was always telling me. Then one day I finds 'er sobbing her little 'eart out, right 'ere in this room, it was, and she tells me she's going to 'ave a baby, and that Lord P don't want 'er no more because she'll be fat and ugly. And 'e can't abide fat women.'

'That's wicked!' cried Grace. 'Especially if it was his baby. Why, he made her like that! Are you sure of this, Mrs Bundle? He seemed such a kind man to me.' Slowly Grace began to apply rouge to her cheekbones. 'When did this Kaye leave the theatre, and where did she go to have the baby? Kathy only came back to the village when Sammy was two months old. What did she do in the meantime?'

The dresser shrugged. 'Don't know where she went. She stayed 'ere a little while and then vanished. Just like that. I 'oped she 'adn't made for the river, right worried about 'er, I was. 'Aven't you got no 'ome, I says to 'er once, no parents, nor family wot'll take you in? Only a grandma, she says, and she won't want me now, not wiv the baby and all. So I tells 'er to come to me for a bit, so she kin sort herself out, like, and I gives 'er my address. But she never comes, Miss Grace, and I never seed 'er again. But I'm certain that were your friend Kathy.'

Grace was certain, too. But she was determined to allow Lord Pridmont to tell his side of the story before she condemned him. And she would have to go carefully, for she needed him to agree to provide for Sammy, to bear responsibility for the poor, motherless child.

'Did this Kaye actually say that Lord Pridmont was the father of her baby?' Grace asked hurriedly, as she heard footsteps outside in the passage and two of the girls burst into the room, whispering and laughing.

'She didn't never say who the man was,' returned Mrs Bundle, helping the girls off with their outer clothing. 'But she was always wiv that Lord P and I never saw 'er wiv any other gentleman.'

On Friday, after the play had ended and the other girls had left the dressing-room, Grace took great care over her appearance. She wore the white brocaded gauze, which she had not worn since Lord Jaspar bought it for her, and piled her hair high on top of her head, holding it in place with numerous pins and two large tortoiseshell combs. Mrs Bundle then placed sprigs of yellow and white flowers amongst the curls on her crown.

When Grace stood up she was somewhat alarmed by the round neckline which was lower than anything she had previously worn, but no amount of pulling or tugging would raise the material nearer to her chin.

'It's indecent, that's wot,' declared the dresser, flinging the black satin cloak around Grace's shoulders in an endeavour to hide her nakedness. 'Wot would your pa say seein' you like that?'

Grace felt the blood rush to her cheeks and she turned towards the mirror, touching her hair with assumed carelessness. Once the greasepaint was removed she looked pale and rather tired, and she wished that she had the courage to re-apply some paint to her cheeks.

'Do not nag me,' she chided. 'This gown was chosen by your precious Lord Ede. I do not care for his taste, but it is too good to throw away and you must admit that the material is lovely.' Grace turned and looked at Mrs Bundle. 'Do not forget that I am doing all this for Samuel. I am quite determined that he shall have a proper start in life, and the only way he will get that is if Lord Pridmont acknowledges him, as his son.'

Unbidden came the thought of Richard Mercury into her mind; he was often in her thoughts these days. How wonderful if he should fall in love with her, and they could marry and live close by. Grace had grown very fond of the baby and would feel a terrible sense of personal loss if he were completely removed from her life. But if she and Richard — Mr Mercury, that was — could live in a house in London, and see the little boy at regular intervals, why, that would be like a fairy tale come true.

'Hurry up, Miss Grace, now do. Me feet are killing me an' I want to go 'ome.' Mrs Bundle spoke irritably, worried about the girl yet knowing that she could do nothing to prevent her going out that night. 'You look lovely and no doubt Lord P and that Mr

Mercury will think so, too. But don't forget your pa, dearie, nor your proper upbringing, neither. It's always the ones from decent backgrounds wot seem to get into the worst troubles, don't ask me why.' She clinked the keys in her hand and stared impatiently at Grace, who was still fiddling nervously with her hair. 'Now leave it alone, dearie, them flowers look lovely and I want to lock up. Hurry up, Miss Grace, it's time we went.'

'I'm going.' Grace moved quickly away from the mirror, pulling the cloak tightly around her body. 'Goodnight, Mrs Bundle, see you tomorrow.' She went past the dresser and down the long stone corridor which led to the top of the stairs.

★ ★ ★

'You look magnificent, my dear,' said Lord Pridmont, reclining on a sofa with his usual mound of cushions behind him.

They were in a different room this time, a Chinese room, filled with vases and lacquered screens and small tables inlaid with mother-of-pearl. There were beautiful wall hangings of embroidered dragons and long-tailed, exotic birds, and a peacock-blue carpet lay upon the floor.

'I chose the Blue Room this evening,' said her host, himself clad in a blue tunic which hung to his knees from a narrow, stand-up collar around his thick neck. Across his chest was emblazoned a scarlet dragon and on his bare feet were a pair of blue satin slippers.

Richard Mercury, Grace was thankful to see, wore a black dress-coat and striped trousers, with only a blue silk cravat about his neck to add colour to his appearance.

'I believe I have some news for you, sir,' Grace said, once she had seated herself on the high-backed chair facing Lord Pridmont. She felt at ease in this room, finding it pleasant to sit on a proper chair to make conversation. 'It has come to my knowledge that my friend Kathy, about whom I spoke last time, if you remember, assumed the name of Kaye Fair for the stage.'

At the mention of this name both men looked instantly alert and Pridmont leaned forward, planting his fat little hands on his knees and gazing at her with intense concentration.

'Kaye Fair?' he said. 'Why, of course we knew little Kaye. Gracious me, do you mean to tell us that she was the poor girl who brought Samuel to your village and then passed away?'

Grace nodded. 'Oh, do please help him, your lordship. Give him a proper education and a good start in life. I am sure he must be your son, and there is nothing for him in Windhaven.'

'Now, now, not so fast, little lady.' Pridmont held up one of his bejewelled hands. 'Naturally I wish to help you, sweet girl, and I shall, I shall. But to presume that I am the father of young Samuel is going a bit far. How can such a matter be proved, Miss Grace? The child might be the offspring of any man in London. How can I know if he is *my* son?'

'But Kathy said Lord P.' Grace stared at the fat man and was suddenly less sure of herself. If his lordship denied being the boy's father, how could she gainsay him?

'I do not deny that I admired the girl's looks, and that we enjoyed her company. We did, did we not, Rich?' The young man nodded slowly. 'But that is a very long way from admitting to being a parent.' Lord Pridmont chuckled. 'Your friend was a very pretty creature, Miss Grace. There must be something in the country air which breeds loveliness, but I dare say she was admired by many gentlemen, and I would not wish to spend money on a boy who was not of my flesh and blood.'

You helped Richard Mercury, she longed to say . . . And he was no relation of yours. But that would have been impertinent and she did not want to antagonise him.

'Mrs Bundle, that is the dresser at the theatre, she says Kathy only spoke about you, that she was very fond of you, sir. I do not believe that she would have given her affection to any other gentleman beside yourself.'

'Well, now, Miss Grace, this is something which can never be decided. I am unsure, and you were not here at the time. And an old theatrical dresser cannot be relied upon to speak the truth, I fear. So, no, I will not accept that this boy is mine. And I may also add that being a man of great wealth, I have to be extraordinarily careful about any claims which are made upon me. Do you understand?'

Dumbly Grace nodded. She knew that Kathy would not have lied, and she believed that Lord Pridmont was Samuel's father. But somewhere, deep inside, she felt a flicker of doubt. Lord Pridmont was so exceptionally ugly, could Kathy really have lain in his arms and allowed him to make love to her? Grace had no clear idea of how a man and woman loved each other, but she knew that it involved close contact, a touching of bodies, and she shivered at the thought of this repulsive old man and her friend.

His lordship's voice broke in upon her troubled thoughts.

'However, I have been most taken with you, my sweet Miss Grace, and have decided upon a plan which should suit us all admirably. I shall care for Samuel, as my ward — '

'Oh, sir!' Grace sat forward on her chair, clasping her hands to her bosom. 'I can never thank you enough!' Relief streamed through her in a rush of warmth. 'I am so grateful and — '

'And you shall come too, and be spoilt and cherished also.'

'Beg pardon, sir?' Grace's mouth fell open and she stared in complete bewilderment at the fat blue figure on the sofa.

'What his lordship is saying,' remarked

Richard Mercury, smiling at her bemused face, 'is that both of you shall come here to live, and he will promise to care for the two of you. It is a splendid arrangement, Miss Grace, and one which I most heartily endorse.' His eyes caressed her as she turned to look at him, shocked into silence by what she had just heard.

'I shall care for you both,' repeated Lord Pridmont, his mouth disappearing as his cheeks and chin bulged in a smile. 'You shall be my responsibility also, and once that silly play has finished its run you must join me here at Cavendish Square.'

'But Father!' Grace burst out, saying the first thing which came into her head. 'Father would never allow it.'

'I shall write to your father explaining the situation. In fact, I might well drive down to see him. It will be a most proper arrangement, my dear Miss Grace, and perhaps some poor folk in your village will also benefit by my patronage?'

A multitude of thoughts flooded

Grace's brain; thoughts of clothing and new roofs for some of the cottagers; a life of luxury for herself and Sammy, and the friendship — perhaps more — of Richard Mercury.

'Leave us, Rich,' commanded Lord Pridmont. 'I wish to speak to Miss Grace on her own.'

Mercury obediently rose and bowed to Grace before leaving the room.

What now? thought the girl wildly. How do I cope with this situation? What shall I answer to his proposition? Does he mean marriage, or will it be a kind of adoption? She shivered, uncertain and a little afraid.

'Come here, little girl, and sit by me. I wish to speak to you and cannot keep shouting across the room.' His lordship swung his short legs to the ground and patted the sofa beside him.

Hesitantly Grace left her chair and went to sit beside the old man.

'That is better. Now, cuddle up close and let us have a little chat. You are a beautiful girl and I want to protect you from the hungry wolves whom I know to be lurking in the shadows. Those such as that scoundrel, Ede, waiting to devour my pretty Grace.'

Lord Pridmont placed a heavy arm around her shoulders and Grace felt his hand, warm and moist, through the flimsy material of her gown. She was repulsed by his closeness, by the dead white dough of his skin, by his tiny black eyes which were peering avidly into her face, by his breath which smelt foul at such close proximity.

Grace closed her eyes, feeling faint. She wanted to escape, to leave the awful old man at once. Why had Richard Mercury left her to face this unpleasant situation on her own? She opened her eyes and looked towards the door, praying that he might appear to save her further embarrassment. She did not know how to talk to Lord Pridmont, had not the experience to deal with his over-friendly attitude. Should she stay and accept his proposal? Or should she fling away every hope of good fortune for herself and Samuel and reject him?

'There, there, my little beauty.' Lord Pridmont began to stroke her neck and his fingers travelled upwards to her hair and fumbled with the pins and combs. Suddenly the combs were pulled away, and the heavy tresses of her red hair came tumbling down, pins falling onto her lap and onto the floor, and her hair falling in shimmering waves about her shoulders, half-covering her heaving bosom.

'Exquisite,' murmured his lordship, putting his face against her hair and nuzzling into her breast.

Grace's mouth was dry with fear and she could feel her heart thumping against her bodice. Dear God, she thought frantically, what was to be done? How could she get away with dignity? She tried to withdraw but the man's arm was firm about her, and his weight was heavy against her side.

'You are going to come here and be my sweet companion, are you not? I rather think that you admire Rich, eh?' Pridmont raised his head and she was forced to look at him with the tell-tale blood suffusing her neck and face. 'Ah, I see that I am right. Well, my dear, you are both beautiful and intelligent, and it would not surprise me if you formed an attachment for each other. It would delight us both to have you here, and Samuel, your little baby, can you imagine what a happy childhood he will have?'

Lord Pridmont sat up straight, bringing his other hand up to touch her rounded cheek. 'Forgive me for admiring you,' he said in a whisper, 'but your skin is perfect, and most unusual for one who must wear that dreadful paint on her face for several hours every day.'

He began stroking her cheek, running his hand very lightly over her flesh, tracing the line of her jaw, her full soft mouth, and her neck. Then he allowed his hand to move further down to explore the swell of her breasts.

Grace caught her breath, struggling

to pull away from his touch, but Pridmont held her firmly, and she saw a little trickle of saliva run down his chin as his hand slipped beneath her bodice and closed upon her breast, fingering her nipple.

'And these — these virgin fruits — surely ripe for the taking.' He lowered his head and she cried out in shock as his tongue ran wetly across her exposed skin.

'How dare you! Let me go!' She screamed at him, hitting out at his bent head, knocking his turban as she did so. The headgear slipped to one side and then fell to the floor, and Grace saw to her horror that his lordship was completely bald.

Anger and terror gave her strength and she thrust him away from her and sprang to her feet, but not before he made a lunge at her and tore the material of her bodice almost to the waist.

Clutching at her ruined gown with one hand, and holding up her skirts with the other, Grace sped across the room and flung open the door, as his lordship sprawled on the sofa behind her, roaring out a string of curses at her departing back. She pushed aside the astonished footman who was waiting in the corridor, and flew down the stairs, gasping for breath as the tears began to flow down her cheeks.

'Let me out!' she shouted at another footman who moved forward in the hall to bar her way. 'Open that door and let me out, damn you!'

Grace shoved him in the chest, as wild as a frenzied cat, and in the face of such ferocity the man tumbled back leaving her free to grasp the door handle and open the door.

Down the steps and out into the street she fled, her mind panic-stricken and racing with terrified thoughts. Would he send after her? Which way should she go? If only she could see a constable and beg for his help!

She ran like a mad woman into the night, with her hair streaming behind her, and it was only as the air made her skin goose-pimple with cold that she realised she had no cloak, and that her appearance must be dishevelled and highly suspect.

Grace paused for a moment beneath a gas lamp, sobbing for breath and putting her fists to her eyes like a weary child. She was very tired and emotionally ravaged, and did not know how she was going to make her way through the streets to her lodgings in her present condition.

At that moment a hand was laid about her shoulders making her scream aloud with fright.

'It is all right, Miss Grace, it is only me.'

Lord Jaspar Ede stood staring grimly down at her, and Grace was so relieved to see him that she flung herself against his broad chest and burst into a torrent of weeping. Lord Jaspar's arms enfolded her, and Grace felt that she had never felt so warm and safe in all her life.

'Come,' said his lordship, 'my carriage is just around the corner. Let me see you home and you can tell me all about it.'

His tone was deep with concern and he helped the girl along the street, his arm about her half-naked shoulders. If Pridmont had harmed one hair of her head he would kill the rat, he thought, glancing down at Grace's wan little face and tousled red hair. Then he averted his eyes quickly from the sight of one bare white breast.

'Here we are, get in and you'll soon be warm and comfortable.'

Ede opened the door of his carriage, bundled her in, spoke a few words to his coachman, and then followed Grace inside. Lord Jaspar wrapped a rug around her and held her firm against his side, trying to ease the shivering of her body, and the flow of tears which continued to trickle down her face.

'Here, mop yourself up and tell me one thing.' He handed her his silk handkerchief. 'Did Pridmont, or that reptile, Mercury, harm you in any way?'

Grace was silent, so ashamed of what had happened that she could not speak. She held the handkerchief to her lips and pressed her head further into his lordship's side.

'Grace, I must know.' Lord Jaspar spoke urgently. 'If either of those men has hurt you he must be punished.'

'No,' she whispered, her voice barely audible above the rattling of the wheels over the cobbled street. 'No, he — that is, Lord Pridmont, he wanted to fondle me and — and kiss me — ' She broke off, shuddering at the memory.

'Who tore your gown?'

'That was when I pulled away. I was frightened and disgusted and as I stood up he — he tried to stop me. But it wasn't Mr Mercury,' she went on quickly, 'he was most respectable in his behaviour towards me, always. He was not there at the time — it was only Lord Pridmont and me.'

'Arranged beforehand, I have no doubt,' answered Ede grimly. 'Do not

130

ever go to that house again, Miss Grace, and refuse to have anything more to do with Mercury. Both men are dangerous and I may not be around another time to save you.'

'How did you know that I was there tonight?' She raised her head to look up at his stern profile. 'Or were you just passing?'

'I have been keeping an eye on you all week. Oh, I know that my own behaviour was not particularly honourable,' admitted Ede hastily, 'but I do care for you, my dear, and was worried lest harm befall you. I know how Pridmont and his lackey have behaved towards innocent young females in the past, and once you made their acquaintance and began seeing Mercury after the play ended, I guessed their intention and vowed to watch that house. I saw you go in this evening and was determined to wait until you came out. If not, I was prepared to come in and fetch you.' He gave a short bark of laughter. 'Once one enters the lion's den, one does not often escape.'

'I do not believe that Mr Mercury is wicked,' said Grace softly. 'I trust him. But never, never will I see Lord Pridmont again!'

'All men are dangerous,' said Lord Jaspar quietly, 'and unfortunately, if you parade your body on the stage you lay yourself open to a hazardous existence, my dear Grace. The sooner you are back in the country with your father, the happier I shall be.'

'I shall be glad to go home. London has taught me much but nothing that I wish to remember.' The carriage rolled to a halt outside her lodgings in Cecil Street. 'Thank you, sir. I shall always be grateful for your kindness.'

Grace gave his lordship a watery smile and pulled the rug more firmly around her. It would not do for Mrs Luce to see her in this state. Hopefully, the woman had gone to bed. If she retired before Grace came home from the theatre, Mrs Luce left the back door open and the girl locked up when she went in.

'Am I forgiven then?' Lord Jaspar stood on the pavement and helped Grace to alight. 'Will you forget all that happened that night at my house? And will you dine with me again?'

She dimpled, lowering her lashes which appeared dark and spiky, still damp from her recent tears. Ede's heart leapt and he longed to lean forward and press his lips against her eyelids. But the girl had been shocked and abused and must be treated very gently in future. He had become astonishingly fond of her and wanted to protect her. One day he would love her, but she was not to be frightened or rushed in any way. It might mean waiting for months, he mused, until the play had ended its run, and he would be forced to make frequent visits into the countryside, and have to face a prudish father into the bargain.

But have her he would, and love and spoil and flatter her until he tired of the game. She was enchanting, and so different to the hard-faced, hard-hearted females who normally trod the boards at the Lane.

Grace had raised her eyes and was looking at him with a mischievous expression on her pale face. 'But no wine, sir?' she queried.

'No wine,' he agreed, smiling.

'Then I shall come, and gladly. Goodnight to you, sir.' She hurried away down the side alley which led to the back of the house.

Joan had not waited up and Grace looked in on her and the baby before going to her own room next door. Both the nurse and the little boy were sleeping peacefully, and it was only as Grace turned away, carrying her candle to the other room, that the thought hit her.

Sammy! She had forgotten all about him in her wild rush to escape Lord Pridmont's clutches. But now the same old question arose to tease her mind. What was to be done about Sammy?

She placed her candle on the table, slipped out of her ruined gown, and had a quick wash before putting on her night-gown. Then she brushed out her tangled mane of hair and plaited it into one long, thick braid down her back, before climbing into bed and blowing out the candle.

Kathy. Sammy. Lord P. These three names chased round and round in her tired brain making it impossible for her to sleep.

Grace had come to London in order to find Samuel's father, and she was convinced that Lord Pridmont was that man, despite his denial. But she had thrown away all hope of a secure future for the little boy by her behaviour tonight. Not that she regretted it.

Grace turned over on her bed and placed her hands beneath her cheek. God forbid that Sammy should grow up in a household dominated by that revolting old man. She was glad that she had found out about him in time. But there still remained the problem of Sammy's future.

Would Granny Lang care for him?

Grace rather doubted if the old woman would be capable of bringing up a small and vigorous boy. And she had no money, besides.

Grace decided that the only thing now would be for her to honour her promise to Kathy and look after the child herself. She frowned into the darkness. There was seldom enough money at home for Father and herself; they seemed always to be wanting for clothes, and did not eat well, either. It had not mattered too much to Grace as she grew up, for she had known no other existence, and threadbare clothing, meagre meals and cold rooms, had seemed faintly unpleasant but something which had to be borne. After all, most of the villagers fared even less well than she and Father did.

But now that she had known a better way of life, now that she had worn fine clothes, had been well fed, and had earned good money for herself, how was she ever going to return to a life of poverty? Yet to stay on in London would be impossible. As Lord Jaspar had so rightly said, London was a dangerous place for a young girl, and she did not wish to try for a part in another play. Once was enough, and all Grace wanted was to return to the fresh air and the safety of rural life.

But there would be another mouth to feed, two, in fact, for Joan would have to remain with her until Sammy was weaned.

Should she marry Tom Laster? Grace knew that he was fond of her and would, with the least encouragement, propose. And Tom's father owned land, nearly fifty acres, and a small herd of cows, and some sheep besides. They lived in their own house on the Downs, just the two men since Mrs Laster died last spring.

Tom could neither read nor write, and Grace knew that she would be marrying beneath her and Father would probably not approve of such a match for his only daughter. But marriage to Tom would mean security for herself and Sammy, and what else was there for her to do?

A clock somewhere struck three times. Grace sighed and turned over again. If only she had not met Richard Mercury. She still believed that he was an innocent pawn in Lord Pridmont's hateful plan. And even Lord Jaspar Ede, with his dark, somewhat foreboding countenance and tall, elegant figure, was a handsome man. If she had never come to London, never set eyes on these two men, she would have settled happily for Tom Laster. But if a husband did things — revolting things like Lord Pridmont tried to do — then she did not think she could bear to be Tom's wife.

Grace buried her face in the pillow, a flood of revulsion flooding through her body. It was a wife's duty to obey her husband, but, oh dear, how hard it would be to comply if she did not love him.

How had Kathy borne to be with Lord P? Grace's eyes flew open in the darkness, remembering her pretty, dainty friend. How could she have loved that dreadful old man? What had possessed her to go with him and accept his attentions? She must talk to Mrs Bundle again; perhaps they were wrong in supposing Lord Pridmont to be Sammy's father. But he had admitted to knowing Kathy, or Kaye, as she had called herself, so it did seem likely that she had been his mistress.

Grace shivered, clenching her fists under the bedcovers, London was an evil place and the sooner she left it the better. Tom might be dirty and uncouth, but he was also gentle and kind, and she knew that she and Sammy would be safe with him. She would have to marry him; there was no alternative.

6

The next few weeks passed quickly. Grace had arranged for Joan to come up and meet her at the theatre every night, unless she was to dine with Lord Ede. Mrs Luce kindly kept an eye on Sammy during the short time that Joan was away from the house, and Grace felt much safer walking home in the girl's company.

Richard Mercury had called once, soon after her escape from Lord Pridmont, and although Grace longed to see him, and to explain that she did not blame him, she had heeded Lord Jaspar's warning and allowed Mrs Bundle to deal with the young man.

'That's that,' said the dresser, smiling grimly as she came back from the door, behind which she had given Mercury the full lash of her rough tongue. ''E'll not be worrying you again, dearie, an' I told 'im that 'e'd 'ave to answer to Lord Jaspar Ede if 'e so much as spoke to you again.'

Grace sighed. 'I do not think he is in any way to blame,' she said softly. 'But as he lives in the same house as Lord P and obviously worships that odious man, it is best if I refuse to see him.'

She was in a confused state of mind these days, and often wished that Kathy had never come back to Windhaven and thus embroiled her in her complicated affairs; with the coming of her friend, Grace's entire world had been turned topsyturvy. In London she had been forced into a new life, a life of great wealth, deceit, lust and superficiality. Grace had spent time with members of the aristocracy and had found them to be untrustworthy; she had learnt to flaunt her body before hundreds of strangers every night, and to wear paint upon her face.

Because of this unnatural way of life she had received endless compliments but everything she did, and much of what she said, was in complete contrast to the way in which she had been taught to behave by her father.

She was finding Lord Jaspar's charms hard to resist, he was so handsome and so very persistent, and she still worried about Sammy and the future which lay ahead of them once they returned to Windhaven.

Fortunately, the play was soon to end and then all decisions would be taken out of her hands. She would return home with Joan and Sammy and then her father could tell her what to do. She would discuss the situation with him and let him decide. At least he was someone who loved her truly, and who possessed impeccable morals. She would abide by his judgement, and if he said Tom, Tom Laster it would have to be.

On Tuesday Grace went shopping straight after lunch, which she had had in her rooms with Joan and Sammy. The following day was Joan's birthday and Grace wanted to buy her a present.

She spent some time in Regent Street trying to decide what to give. She felt guilty about the girl for she had not allowed her to return to the village, as Joan had desired. Grace had the strongest feeling that if she had let Joan go back to Windhaven without her, she would have lost possession of Sammy. The girl would have gone back to her family and become swamped in that filthy existence again, and Grace feared that she would not have given up the little boy when Grace finally returned to claim him.

It was better, therefore, that she keep both nurse and baby with her, and that they all return to Windhaven together. That way Sammy would always be within her control and Joan could be dismissed once the boy was weaned. But Grace knew that Joan was genuinely fond of the baby, and knew, also, that she could never have managed without her in London. So she wanted to buy her something special, to show her gratitude. Eventually, Grace chose a silk kerchief of emerald green, which could be worn over the head, or was large enough to be folded and worn as a shawl upon the shoulders.

When she returned to Cecil Street with her purchase, Grace was startled to see Mrs Luce poking her head out of the front parlour and gazing at her with a strange, half-worried, half-excited expression upon her face. Then she bobbed back and slammed the door without so much as a word. It was especially significant as Mrs Luce never missed the chance to have a chat, finding Grace's life at the theatre, and her friendship with Lord Jaspar Ede, of infinite fascination.

Grace stared at the closed door, shook her head in puzzlement, and then mounted the stairs to the first floor.

'I'm home, Joan!' she called, untying her bonnet and slipping the shawl from off her shoulders. 'Has Sammy been good whilst I've been away?'

She walked through to the nurse's room and found it empty. For a moment her heart skipped a beat, it was most unusual for Joan to go out at this hour of the day, particularly as Grace had said that she would be home for tea, and wished to spend time with Sammy before going to the theatre that evening. But it was a pleasant afternoon, maybe Joan had taken Sammy for a quick outing in the fresh air.

Grace moved back into the sitting-room and as she did so Lord Jaspar appeared in the doorway of her bedroom.

'What are you doing here?' Grace stared in astonishment. He had never visited before, always meeting her at the theatre, and she had refrained from inviting him back to her lodgings being somewhat ashamed of their drabness when compared to his lordship's splendid home in Bedford Square.

'Have you seen Joan and the baby?' she enquired, her mind still occupied with their disappearance.

Lord Jaspar walked purposefully to the door which led out to the stairs and turned the key in the lock. He then dropped the key into his waistcoat pocket.

'I sent the nurse out and gave her a sovereign, telling her not to return until six o'clock. The baby, ma'am, is downstairs with your good landlady.' Ede strode forward and caught Grace by the shoulders as she recoiled from his speech.

'What right have you to come here interfering in my affairs? We may be friends, but this is presumptuous behaviour on your part, sir!' She was shaking with anger.

'Friends no more, my dear Grace. I have played your game long enough and do not enjoy being duped. Your innocent and virtuous behaviour quite convinced me, and made me forget until today that you are an actress and trained to play a part.'

'What do you mean?' Grace beat at his broad chest with her fists. 'Take your hands off me!'

She tried to struggle free from his

grasp but Lord Jaspar was a stronger and fitter man than the obese Lord Pridmont, and with a sinking feeling of despair Grace knew that she was no match for Lord Jaspar Ede.

'Into the bedroom with you,' he said firmly. 'I have neither the time nor the desire for excuses. I have waited for you long enough, ma'am, and have shown patience beyond reason.'

He pushed her before him, closing the bedroom door behind them with his foot.

He must think that Samuel was her child. Had Joan said nothing to explain the situation?

'It is not what you think,' Grace said, turning to face him, her hands clasped to her bosom. 'Sammy is not my child and I have never — '

'Enough!' Lord Jaspar took her into his arms. 'You need lie no more. I have called your bluff and the cards are now upon the table.' He bent and kissed her trembling lips. 'Ah, Grace, you do not dislike me, I know that for certain, and surely I am more attractive than that great slug Pridmont? Forget your acting, sweetheart, and let us enjoy ourselves. You were made for loving, my beauty, and I shall show you how 'tis meant to be done.'

For a moment Grace stood rigid and then, as Lord Jaspar began to kiss her again, slowly and tenderly, she found herself unable to resist his embrace and her limbs began to tremble and lose strength. She felt weak and giddy, and very warm as she lay against his hard body.

The next hour passed in a haze of shock and growing passion. The man used her gently, and Grace realised in a blur of confused emotions that Lord Jaspar was an accomplished lover. Fleetingly she was aware that despite the outrage to her naked body, the act of love was tolerable, in fact almost enjoyable.

When he had finished with her, Ede let out a muffled oath and began pulling on his clothes in feverish haste.

Grace lay sprawled upon the bed, totally spent, ashamed to admit that it was not so very bad, and that she almost wished Lord Jaspar would make love to her all over again.

She watched him dress, admiring his broad shoulders and slim waist, wanting to reach out and kiss one of his long-fingered, beautiful hands.

'Did I please you, sir?' she asked hesitantly, not wanting him to go; willing him to respond kindly, to say that he would see her again, to reassure her that she was desirable.

Ede turned and looked down at her white form on the bed, and at the tangled mass of red hair framing her small face. He saw her mouth, bruised and soft from his kisses, and her eyes, gentle with love and newly-awakened desire. Then he bit his lip and turned upon his heel, shrugging on his top coat as he made for the door. His face was set with anger and he did not speak before leaving her alone in the room.

He was furious with himself and anxious to escape, to leave the vile scene of his conquest far behind. Every word which she had spoken had been true. She was neither a harlot nor a mother, and he had abused her trust and treated her as savagely as the man whom he hated and despised. Ede flung himself out of the room and thundered down the stairs, cursing himself as he ran.

Grace lay still upon the bed, her eyes smarting with unshed tears. She had not pleased him. Lord Jaspar had been gentle and very tender with her, but she had obviously not responded in the right way and had disappointed him.

Once her shock and fear had evaporated beneath his caresses, she had responded with joy. But she realised now, to her shame, that she had fallen in love with a man who no longer respected her, nor desired her, once he had succeeded in seducing her.

★　★　★

At the end of July Grace returned to Windhaven, accompanied by Joan and baby Samuel. She had left Mrs Bundle with a real sense of grief, but there was no one and nothing else in the city of London which she regretted leaving. She had not set eyes on Lord Jaspar Ede again, and had heard Crispin Mellish telling the stage manager that Ede had departed for Italy and would be away for some months.

The Countess From Crewe ended its run, another cast and another producer moved in ready for rehearsals, and Grace Fairweather bade farewell to Drury Lane forever.

She was sick in both mind and body, desperately hurt by Lord Jaspar's rejection of her, and wanted only to return to Windhaven and lick her wounds like some injured animal.

Grace felt tired as well as being depressed, and knew that the late nights and the long and strenuous hours of theatrical life had taken their toll.

At least she was not returning like

Kathy, she told herself fiercely, as she and Joan and the baby rattled southwards on their way to the village. She had met temptation as her friend had done, but she, Grace, had not succumbed to evil forces, and apart from that one devastating experience with Lord Jaspar, she had come through her months in London with her nature unspoilt, and her mind a great deal clearer on many subjects. She was proud of the fact that she had helped to support many people during the past four months, and now she was ready to settle down and lead a more orderly, albeit thrifty, existence.

Her father welcomed her home in his undemonstrative fashion, and once Joan and Sammy were settled into the Vicarage, Grace waited for an appropriate moment and then asked the vicar's advice.

'Shall I make a point of being friendly towards Tom Laster?' she asked hesitantly, as she and her father sat before the kitchen range before making their way to bed. Joan had already gone upstairs with Samuel so this was Grace's chance to speak to her father in private.

'I could stay behind after Matins on Sunday and speak to him.'

'Tom Laster?' Parson Fairweather rubbed his eyes and yawned. 'What would you be wanting with that young oaf?'

'I was thinking of Sammy. As you know, I could not trace his father in London, so now I must plan ahead for his future.'

'I was meaning to talk to you about that, once you had settled down to village life again.' The vicar placed his finger tips together and eyed his daughter gravely over the top of his pointed hands. 'Joan has mentioned to me that she would like to return to her family. Why not let her and the boy go?'

'Because he is not hers!' cried out Grace. 'I promised Kathy that I would be responsible for him. He is my child now, not Joan Crump's.'

Her father grunted. 'Joan has succoured him these last five months and I cannot see what claim you have to him. Besides, he is a bastard, conceived in sin, and I must admit, Daughter, that it grieves me to keep those two beneath my roof. One, an immoral wench whose own illegitimate child died, and the other the misbegotten son of a flighty little actress and some anonymous and debauched aristocrat. It is not seemly to have such beings in the Vicarage, Grace, and I hope that you will accept this fact once you have grown accustomed to our way of life once more.'

'But you cannot lay the sins of the parents upon the shoulders of an innocent child!' Grace retorted angrily. 'Christ taught us to love and to forgive, and especially to care for children. I do not think your attitude is Christian-like, Father.'

Parson Fairweather's colour rose in his white face and his brows drew together over his dark eyes. 'That is no way to speak to your father, girl, but no doubt your months away in London have taught you much that is deplorable and ungodly. I would remind you that I am sheltering and feeding all three of you, and you are beholden to me for everything. You, as my only child, may naturally remain at the Vicarage so long as you retain a civil tongue in your head, but I do not wish to hear talk of Tom Laster.

'As for Samuel Lang, or whatever name he goes by, it is high time he went out of your life. You have become too fond of that infant already, and it is both right and proper for Joan Crump to take him back to her family. Her mother has a brat of the same age so they will be company for each other as they grow older. The Crumps have little money, it is true, but what is another mouth to feed amongst so many?

'Have you thought about my side of the question?' he went on quickly as Grace tried to interrupt. 'How does my authority stand in the village if I am seen to harbour a whore and a bastard beneath my roof? I am forever preaching against fornication and the sins of the flesh, you know that, Grace. Yet here at the Vicarage, I appear to condone immorality.'

The parson shook his greying head vigorously. 'I shall help them when I can, of course, by taking food and clothing, and by talking to them and trying to make them see the error of their ways. I shall never cease fighting for their souls, Grace.' His voice rang out as if he were in his pulpit, bullying the poor, witless, evil-smelling people of his parish. 'But I shall not give them sanctuary here in my house, and the sooner you accept that the happier you will be, my dear.'

Grace sat silently, her head bowed, clasping her hands together on her lap. She would not give Sammy up and watch him go to that filthy hovel occupied by the Crump family.

She would have to meet Tom Laster

in secret; he offered the only hope of salvation. If he would marry her and take on Sammy as his own son, they could all live together in a reasonably comfortable manner.

Her father stood up as she mused, then bent forward and kissed her on the brow. 'Mark my words, Grace, and do as I bid you. You were always a good daughter to me, if somewhat defiant of late. Do not fail me now, I beg you.'

Grace smiled distantly and watched him leave the room. He was getting old and did not walk as upright as he used to. One day he would follow her mother to the grave and then what would happen to her, Grace? Perhaps, if the new clergyman were a single man, she would be allowed to remain on as housekeeper. But it was far more likely that he would arrive with a wife and family, and Grace's services would not be required. What would she do then?

There was nothing for it but to take her chance with Tom Laster, and see if he could be persuaded to marry her. She was sorry to disobey her father, but the young were more important now, and both she and Sammy had to provide for their future. Grace had learnt a great deal in London, as she had told Lord Jaspar —

Her heart leaped at the thought of him and she put him hastily from her mind. She was never going to think about him — never!

After her experience at the Theatre Royal and her lessons with Miss Kelly, she would be a miserable creature if she could not make Tom lose his heart to her. And she would be a good wife to him; she knew now what a female had to do, and she would be loving and obedient and do all that was expected of her. If he would give Sammy and herself a home, she would treat him with undying and loyal devotion.

Grace was glad to have some definite plan in mind; she was still not feeling completely well and would frequently find herself in tears for no reason at all. Her state of health was depressing and rather worrying, but now she could plan ahead and it would give her something to think about other than her silly, weak body.

On Sunday morning, to Grace's relief, her father was busily engaged at the church door in conversation with the doctor and his wife, so she hung back after the service and allowed the rest of the congregation to pass her on their way out to the porch. In one of the rear pews she saw Tom Laster waiting his turn to file out.

Grace smiled and moved forward to greet him. He was a big, wide-shouldered lad, with unruly hair neatly slicked down for church, and eyes a very bright blue in his weatherbeaten face.

'Hello, Tom, how nice to see you again. I have been away in London but now I've come home for good. Did you miss me?'

She fluttered her lashes and watched

his neck redden above his stiff, Sunday best collar.

'London, Miss Grace? That's a good long way, and all.'

He stared down at her animated little face, bemused by such feminine prettiness. His eyes travelled over her lilac velvet morning dress and soft grey cashmere shawl, topped by the matching hat with the large silver bow.

This was the only outfit which Grace had allowed herself to keep. All the other gowns and slippers, petticoats and shawls, had been sold to the other girls at the theatre. Grace had not asked much for the clothing, the girls were careful with their pence, not knowing when they would be in work again, but none could resist the expensive materials and elegant designs which Lord Jaspar had chosen for his protégé.

Now Tom stood gazing at her in awe, twisting his cap between his work-worn hands, his tongue silent.

'Do you still go to Granny Lang's?' asked Grace softly. 'Shall I see you there this afternoon? I have so much to tell you, Tom, such adventures, you'll not believe them!'

Tom remained speechless, and Grace wished that he would answer. Out of the corner of her eye she could see the crowd of parishioners thinning out, and at any moment her father might look back into the church and see her there with the lad.

'Will you come, Tom?'

'I'll be there, Miss Grace.' Tom paused, he was a slow-moving, slow-thinking countryman and would not be hurried. 'But I shan't stay long. My Dad, he's not too well at present.'

'I am sorry to hear that but tell me more when we meet,' said Grace swiftly. 'Now I must go and look for my gloves, I left them in the pew.'

She scuttled away back down the aisle, allowing the young man to join the tail end of the congregation and leave the church without her.

The afternoon visit was not a success from Grace's point of view, for Granny Lang asked all the questions, whilst Tom sat silent, wanting to know about the theatre, and life in London, and whether she had found out anything about Kathy's past life there, and why she had not been able to trace Samuel's father. Grace did not mention Lord Pridmont's name, the episode in Cavendish Square had been so unpleasant and frightening that she wanted to forget it, and she did not speak of Lord Jaspar, either. Memories of her stay in London were mostly painful so she was hard pressed to find enough interesting and trivial facts to appease the old woman's curiosity.

Tom scarcely spoke a word, but he watched Grace intently, and she knew that she could make him fall in love with her if only she had enough time, and the right opportunity. But with her father's unhelpful and disdainful attitude towards the farm lad, she knew that she had a difficult task ahead of her.

'I'll be staying one more week and then I'm going back to my ma's and Sammy's going with me.' Joan confronted Grace with the unwelcome news that evening when she arrived back from Granny Lang's.

Parson Fairweather was at Evensong and although Grace always accompanied him for this service, which she loved best of all, she had excused herself this evening on account of a headache. So she was sitting, with Sammy on her knee, waiting for the throbbing in her temples to ease, as Joan made her announcement.

The kitchen, with its big range, was the only warm room in the house, despite its uneven flagged floor and the draughts which whistled in under the doors and swelled the drawn curtains on windy days. The kitchen was where everyone congregated when there was no work to be done, and Grace always chose the rocking chair which had been her mother's. It soothed her with its gentle motion.

'I cannot allow you to go yet, or to take the baby with you.' Grace frowned up at the girl, who stood in an aggressive pose before her, head thrust forward from her shoulders, hands on hips. 'And I cannot understand why you should *want* to return to your mother's. You are far more comfortable here, and cleaner, and better fed.' Grace was put out by Joan's attitude and still worrying about how she could see more of Tom Laster.

'I miss my ma,' said Joan, 'and she misses me. When I were in London course I couldn't be with her, but now it's stupid to be in the same village and live just up the road from her. The two babies will be company for each other, and Ma needs my help with the young 'uns. Besides,' she flashed an ominous look at Grace from her sly brown eyes, 'besides, there's only place for one babe in this house. Can't see your father welcoming two screaming brats.'

'I don't know what you mean.' Grace caught at Sammy's hand which was trying to pull a strand of her hair, and held it to her heart. 'I don't expect you to bring your mother's child up here, as well. I only ask you to go on caring for Sammy, as you have always done, and you can visit your home whenever you wish.'

'You don't understand me, miss, I said *you* was going to have a baby. Didn't mean me Ma's!' She smiled without humour and reached for Sammy. 'Time for a feed,' she said.

Grace's attention was fixed on the girl opposite and all other thoughts left her mind. It could not be true! Not after that once with Lord Jaspar — such things did not happen so quickly.

'You are mistaken, Joan,' she said in a tightly-controlled voice, giving the little boy to the wet nurse and then putting her hands quickly on to her lap, trying to hide the quivering of her fingers beneath the folds of her skirt. 'You have a nasty suspicious mind and I do not

165

wish to hear any more of that kind of talk.'

'Oh, no, I'm not mistaken, miss.' Joan sat down in the sagging armchair and opened her bodice. 'I know the signs — bin through it meself and seen my ma Gawd knows how often in the very same condition. What you missed — one, two months, is it?' She peered over at Grace as the baby nestled against her, one fist kneading at her full breast. 'Reckon it'll be here in the Spring, and we're best away now. Don't care to think about the reverend's anger. But you've got to expect that, miss, he won't be happy, will he?'

Grace sat in stunned silence. It was true that her body had not been functioning normally for a couple of months, but she had put that down to weariness, and the terrible sense of loss which had afflicted her after Lord Jaspar's departure. But she was not putting on weight — she clung wildly to that fact.

'It's all nonsense, Joan,' she said, her

voice sounding high and strident in the quiet room. 'I can wear all my clothes, in fact the waists are quite loose on me. I have *lost* weight, I tell you, and you have an evil mind. Shame on you for having such an opinion of me!'

Joan nodded sagely, in no way put out by her companion's fury. 'It's usual to be a bit thin early on, then suddenly — oops! You'll be putting on like anything. I *know*, Miss Grace, it's no use thinking to deceive me.'

With a feeling of desperation Grace rose to her feet and went quickly from the room. She ran upstairs and flung herself down upon the bed.

Dear God, she prayed, forcing a fist against her weeping mouth, what now? What in heaven should she do now?

★ ★ ★

The following week Joan departed, taking Samuel with her. There was nothing Grace could do to stop her,

167

and she watched the girl leave the Vicarage with agony in her heart.

She would get Sammy back one day. She would! As soon as he was weaned and Grace had sorted out her own future, she would claim the little boy. He was hers. She had promised Kathy that she would care for her son, and Joan Crump had no right to him.

But Grace could say nothing at present. Joan knew her terrible secret and would have told Parson Fairweather the truth if Grace had made a scene about her leaving.

Desperately, Grace sought about in her mind for the best way of breaking the news to her father, only there was no best way. There was no way of beautifying the blatant, ugly truth.

The parson, in his stiff, unemotional way, was pleased to see the back of the slatternly girl and the baby which had taken up too much of his daughter's time and affection. Now Grace would be at home for him, alone; cleaning his house, cooking for him, and helping him in his work with the sick and needy.

But Grace withdrew into herself, becoming distrait in mind and speech. She was not the admiring listener which the clergyman had hoped for when expounding his dictatorial views, or rehearsing his sermons. His daughter was pale and listless, totally lacking in attention towards him. At first he put her mood down to depression, an understandable feeling at the loss of the boy-child. But as the weeks passed and Grace became ever more withdrawn, Parson Fairweather became impatient.

He made her pray with him, both mornings and evenings, kneeling on the cold stone floor of the kitchen, without a cushion for her knees, or support for her body. His voice would drone on and on in her ears until Grace wondered for how long she could bear it without screaming.

Then, one day in early November, two things happened. She fainted away on the cold flags in the middle of a particularly long litany, which annoyed her father more than usual. And at mid-day he returned to the Vicarage, with his face as grey and hard as a block of hewn granite. He found Grace standing at the sink in her faded blue velvet gown, a white apron around her waist, peeling potatoes for their lunch.

She turned at his entrance in some surprise for he was earlier than usual. One look at his face was enough for her to guess the worst. Very slowly and carefully she dried her chapped hands upon her apron and listened to what he had to say.

'I have just heard a most terrible rumour and I demand to know the truth from your own lips.' His dark eyes swept over her figure, resting for a moment on her waist, where the folds of her skirt bulged slightly beneath her apron. 'Are you with child?'

Grace lifted her head, her face whiter than ever, in startling contrast to the red of her hair and the burning glow of her sore hands.

'Yes, Father,' she said quietly.

The veins on the man's temples bulged with anger and she wondered for a moment if his head could bear the strain, or if he would fall senseless to the floor at her feet. His mouth opened and shut, yet no sound issued from his dry lips.

'I am sorry you had to hear it in such a way, but I could not think how to break it to you,' she whispered.

'May God damn you to all eternity.' The words came at last, harsh and croaking; froth appeared at the corner of the parson's twisted mouth, and he brought one of his fists crashing down on the table before him. 'To think that a daughter of mine is nothing better than a common whore! Get out of this house — at once — do you hear?'

He strode forward, round the end of the table, cuffing at her head with his clenched fist. 'You are no longer of my family, and will never set foot in this house again. Out, I say!' He caught her by the shoulders as she flinched away from him, and pushed her towards the door. 'Get out this instant!'

Parson Fairweather pushed his daughter before him, out into the passage which led to the front door, and with every word his movements became more violent, making her head rock upon her shoulders.

'I have lived in this village for the past thirty years. I have preached constantly against filth and fornication, and have endeavoured to purge all vice and lust from the hearts and minds of the people who would practise such abominations. And now my own daughter, flesh and blood of my dear departed wife, has *dared* to flout my teaching! Has dared to come back here into my house and bring her vile, unclean body into my presence. If I were not a man of God, I'd kill you for this!'

He gave her a final shake which threw her sideways so that she hit her head against the door post.

'You are mad!' gasped Grace, putting a trembling hand to her head. When she lowered her hand she saw that there was blood on her fingers. 'Let me be and I'll gladly go. But I must collect my things — let me go upstairs and fetch a few — '

'You'll fetch nothing!' The parson towered over her, his eyes blazing with unholy wrath. 'There is the door — go!'

Grace crouched back against the door frame, terrified of the hatred which burnt black in her father's eyes. 'I must get my shawl. Please Father, let me get my shawl.'

'You'll take nothing from here. Out, I say, and fend for yourself, you whore!'

He gave her a last shove out onto the porch, and then the door was slammed in her face and she heard the key turn in the lock.

There was a cold wind blowing and grey clouds scudded across the sky. Grace removed her apron and wrapped it around her shoulders for warmth. Then she folded her arms across her bosom and began walking quickly up the lane towards the Downs. Tom must help her now. There was nowhere else to turn, no one else to whom she could go for help. Granny Lang was too old and besides, she had been through all this turmoil once before. Grace could not disturb the tranquillity of her old age for a second time.

She was beginning to feel sick and shaky from the blow to her head, and she feared for the life of her unborn child. Dazedly, as if in a dream, she dragged her tired legs up the hill to the gate at the end of the lane. Then she entered the first field and began the long slow haul over the spongy turf in the direction of the Lasters' farmhouse.

After ten minutes it began to rain, a fine slanting rain, which struck fear into the girl's already frightened heart. If she could not get warm and dry quickly, her baby would surely die within her womb.

When Grace eventually knocked on the sturdy oak door she felt close to death herself. Tom Laster found her on her knees, soaked to her very skin, the gown of her once blue velvet, saturated black, and the white apron hanging like a wet rag about her neck. With an exclamation of shocked dismay, Tom lifted her in his arms and carried her into the house.

7

Several days were to pass before Grace was fully aware of her surroundings. Sometimes she was conscious of hands tending her, of soup being spooned into her mouth, and of voices, both male and female. Once she thought she heard a baby crying, and wondered if her child had been born without her knowing it. But it was too early for that — much too early.

Slowly she dragged her numb senses back to consciousness and the first thing she saw was Joan Crump's face.

'Awake, are you? About time, too. Poor Mister Laster's bin that worried about you.'

There was no sympathy in Joan's voice, but it made Grace blink and try to sit up.

'That'll do. No good tiring yourself and making more trouble for me. Lie still and I'll get you a cup of tea.'

Grace lay still and looked about the room. She was in a big bed, far wider than her narrow bed at home, and the ceiling above her was low and raftered. There was one small window, diamond-paned, and through it she could make out the swell of the Downs beyond. She was in the Lasters' farmhouse, safe for the time being.

Grace gave a little sigh and realised thankfully that she was warm and comfortable, and there was no pain. She put her hands to her stomach and felt the curve of her belly beneath the flannel nightgown. Thank God the baby was still there! Even as her hands smoothed the shape, she felt a slight bulge on her right side, and then a decided kick.

She smiled and went on stroking her stomach. They had both survived their terrifying ordeal and were safe at last. She must see Tom and thank him, but for him she might not have been alive at this moment.

But what was Joan doing here? And Sammy? Grace heaved herself up a few inches in the bed and pulled the pillows closer beneath her shoulders. Where was Sammy?

The door opened and Joan came in bearing a tray. She placed it on the table beside the bed, then leaned across and hoisted Grace further up into a sitting position.

'Here, drink this. The sooner you can be up and about the better for all of us.'

Grace sipped at the hot, sweet tea. 'What are you doing here?' she asked. 'Is Sammy with you?'

''Course he is — Ma can't feed two. And Mister Laster called and asked me to come up and help. In a fair old tizzy, he was. What with his Dad ill, and you sick, and the farm to cope with. So I've come and I'll care for his Dad until he's better. You should be all right in a day, or two. Then, I don't know. Planning on staying, are you, Miss Grace?'

Her dull brown eyes looked at Grace without emotion. 'The pious old parson threw you out, did he? Now that's not Christian, is it, miss? What you going to do when the baby comes? You going back to London to all them fancy gentlemen?'

'Goodness me, Joan, so many questions!' Grace put her free hand to her head. 'Give me time to think. I don't know what I'm going to do but I'll speak to Tom when I feel stronger and we'll work something out, I'm sure.'

'Well, don't go adding to his worries. He's got enough with his Dad bad, and all.'

Joan picked up the tray and walked to the door.

'Can I see Sammy?' Grace called after her.

'Maybe tomorrow, when I've time. Got to see to the old man now. Can't keep stopping and chatting, I've work to do.' She went out and the door swung to behind her.

Later that day, towards nightfall, Tom came to Grace's room. He stood hesitantly in the doorway, looking across at her with his gentle blue eyes.

'Joan said you was feeling better, Miss Grace. I'm right glad to hear it — in a terrible state, you was, when I found you on the doorstep.'

'Thank you, Tom. I believe you saved my life, and that of my baby.' Grace smiled at the young man, wishing that he would take the initiative for once. 'Please come and sit down, I want to talk to you.'

She patted the bed, but Tom Laster's face became redder and he tiptoed across the room in his stockinged feet and brought a chair forward on which he perched himself, several feet from the bed.

'Tell me what happened,' Grace said. 'I remember coming here in the rain — it was dreadful!' She shivered, thinking of the cold, and the wind, and the slope which went up and up before her eyes in a never-ending rise. 'For how long have you been sheltering me?'

'You came — ' he paused, staring up at the ceiling and counting on his thick, stubby fingers — 'you came a week ago last Thursday, and I didn't rightly know what to do, Miss Grace.' He grinned bashfully, clasping and unclasping his fingers. 'We do have Dolly to help in the mornings, but it didn't seem right having a nice young lady like you with only me and Dad here nights. Then Dolly says about Joan, and her being used to you, like, so I goes down to call her.

'And I'm ever so glad she came, Miss Grace, because that Saturday Dad were took bad — can't move at all now, he can't, and the doctor says he's got to have someone with him all the time. And I'm in the fields and round the farm, so it's a good job Joan's here and can look after both of you.'

He let out a deep sigh and grinned again. 'Nice having the house full,' he said. 'Not bin like this since Ma was took. And now there's you and Joan and little Sammy, and I'm right glad you came, Miss Grace. You done the right thing coming here.'

Grace stared across at the young man with the clear blue eyes and corn-coloured hair. 'Why, Tom Laster,' she exclaimed, 'I have never heard you say so much in your life before. Company *must* be good for you!'

He laughed and shuffled his stockinged feet on the floorboards. 'Joan and me, we talk most evenings by the fire, and I reckon it's bin good for me. Dad, he's a quiet man, see? Don't hold with chatter — not unless there's something special needs saying, and since Ma died he's bin worse.' Tom paused, frowning slightly. 'Don't know if he'll ever talk again now. Real bad, he is, Miss Grace. But Joan'll look after him — keep him warm and comfortable, the doctor says.'

Grace did not care for all this talk about Joan. It was high time she got up and made her presence felt in the house. She had been able to make Tom laugh in the old days, and she would do it again, sitting around the fire in the evenings. That sounded nice and cosy, but she wished that Joan was not there.

'You know the reason my father threw me out, Tom?' she said carefully. 'I want you to know the truth.'

'Yes, Miss Grace, Joan said.' He went red again and wiggled his toes.

'There is no need to go into the whole sad story now,' she went on quickly, 'but I want you to know, Tom, that — that I was taken against my will.'

Grace shut her eyes, remembering. It had happened against her will, hadn't it? Suddenly Lord Jaspar's face rose up in her mind as vividly as a painted picture, and she saw his amused, gold-flecked eyes, and his springy black hair which would not lie flat, and his firm mouth which seldom smiled but when it did, lightened his face with a devastating charm.

'Joan told me,' Tom muttered, breaking into her thoughts.

Grace's eyes flew open. 'Joan has told you a great deal about me, hasn't she? But I assure you that I am a good and honourable female and would *never* give myself freely to a man out of wedlock.'

'I know, I know, Miss Grace, now don't take on.' He stood up and carried his chair back to the corner, where he placed it carefully against the wall. 'You're not to go upsetting yourself. You are to stay here all nice and quiet and not get up, see? Not till the doctor says.'

'When is he calling again?' She wanted to get up, wanted to be about the house doing her fair share of the duties.

'He comes by Tuesdays and Saturdays, he'll be round tomorrow. Now go to sleep, Miss Grace, and don't you fret. Everything's going to be all right.'

Tom tiptoed out, leaving Grace staring mutinously at the door.

★　★　★

In the days that followed Grace was allowed downstairs, and was reunited with Sammy, to their mutual joy. He was almost walking now and was a golden-haired cherub, with huge blue eyes and an enchanting smile. He was a contented child and Grace adored him, playing with him, and singing to him, most of the day, whilst Joan scurried about with tight lips and darting, unfriendly eyes.

Unfortunately for Grace, she did not have the strength she had once possessed and she tired easily, so she was unable to help with many of the household tasks. But she prepared the food for all their meals, sitting as much as possible at the big, scrubbed table in the huge kitchen, and she polished the brass and kept Sammy out of Joan's and Dolly's way. He was almost weaned, and as Grace had so much time for him he made his preference for her company increasingly obvious.

Joan, Grace had to admit, was turning into an excellent housewife. She and Dolly did not get on too well together, the latter resenting Joan's sudden appearance at the farm. But no doubt the younger girl put the old servant to shame, for her strong, stocky body was never still, and she ran up and down the stairs tending the sick man, and also found time to dust and clean areas which had obviously not been touched since Mrs Laster died.

Grace kept out of the way as much as possible, and grew steadily bigger and heavier and slower. With the shorter evenings, Tom would come in earlier at night, but Grace was so weary by the end of the day that she retired to bed, leaving Joan to provide the cosy chats beside the fire.

Yet despite the many disadvantages of her condition, Grace was not dismayed. She knew that she was more attractive than Joan, and she occasionally caught Tom looking at her with the old admiration in his eyes. Once she had had her baby, and her figure was back to its normal shape, and her strength and energy had returned, then she knew she would be able to claim Tom's attention, and his heart. At the moment he was very polite to her, very gentle in speech and manner, and rather too formal. Nothing more could be done at present, Grace decided philosophically, and she was thankful that Joan Crump was in the house. Despite Dolly's help in the mornings, Grace knew that she could never have managed the household chores, nor the constant caring for the old man upstairs, until after her baby was born.

Christmas came and went, and there was a brief mild spell in February when Grace felt she could almost smell the spring. One sunny afternoon, when Sammy was having his afternoon nap and Joan was busy upstairs, Grace wandered out of the house and walked a short distance down the hill, before seating herself upon the short-cropped grass. Far below she could see the village of Windhaven and even, if she looked carefully, the chimneys of the Vicarage. But Grace did not want to look; that was all behind her now. Her father had said he never wanted to see her again, there had been no word from him at Christmas time, and she certainly wanted nothing more to do with him, either.

She lifted her face to the sky, feeling at peace. She would wait patiently for the birth of her baby, which was very near now, and then she would set her cap at Tom Laster. Grace smiled at the thought. He was such a dear, simple soul, undemanding and patient, and so kind to people and animals alike. Sammy loved him, and Tom was obviously very fond of the little boy.

Grace placed a comforting hand upon her stomach and gazed unseeingly before her, in passive serenity.

It was a while before she realised that somebody was climbing the hill towards her. Her eyes had been on the distant figure for some time but they had been unfocused, her thoughts far away. Now Grace blinked, and stared at the man who was striding rapidly towards her, taking the slope in long, vigorous steps. As he advanced, her heart began to thump in a frightening combination of fear and excitement. She wanted to leap up and vanish over the brow of the hill behind her, but she was too fat and, indeed, found she could not move at all. Anguish, shock, elation — whatever the emotions were which churned within her body, held her rigid to the grassy knoll as if she were a part of the very earth.

'So, at last I have found you.' Lord Jaspar halted before her, one knee slightly bent, a hand upon his hip, panting slightly as he gazed down at her. 'Good day to you, Miss Grace, and how do you do?'

He wore a claret red dress-coat over fawn-coloured trousers, which were strapped beneath his boots, and a cream frilled shirt. His hat was in his hand and his black hair was tousled and somewhat wild in appearance.

Lord Jaspar let out a gasp of relief and slid down upon the grass beside her. 'I thought I was fit but that climb has proved otherwise. Well, Miss Grace, have you no words of welcome? I've been searching the south of England for you these past weeks, and now that I have found you, you remain obstinately silent. Have you lost your tongue?'

'I do not know what to say.' She put her hands up to her bosom to try and stem the racing of her heart, and stared down at the village below them. 'How did you find me here?'

If she looked at him she would be lost. His voice brought back all those memories she was trying to forget; it was so long since she had heard a cultured voice, and this man's was deep and caressing, with that trace of maddening laughter in it. When she had first met him, Grace had considered Lord Jaspar to be stern, a rather humourless man. But, as she grew to know him better, she felt that for some extraordinary reason, he seemed to find her amusing. And he was so elegantly dressed . . . and his hands and nails would be clean, and his linen spotless, and his hair would smell of that spicy perfumed soap he always used, and his skin . . .

She bent her head suddenly, tears pricking behind her closed eyelids. Why did he have to come? Now when she was so vulnerable. And to see her like this — so ugly and fat and badly dressed. Oh, she could not bear it!

Lord Jaspar did not appear to notice her distress, and began talking calmly, telling her of his adventures.

'I came back to England just after Christmas and decided that it would be pleasant to see you again, but you had vanished without trace,' he said. 'There is another play on at the Lane, and different girls now clatter up and down those stone passages and inhabit the dressing-rooms. Crispin Mellish is tucked away in his house on Hampstead Heath, working away on some new idea, and had no notion of where you might have gone, and Mrs Luce has moved out of London so I could not question her. Dearie me,' he sighed, and plucked at a blade of grass, 'it was all most inconvenient.'

Grace could not help smiling, although she kept her head turned away from him. To think that she had caused Lord Jaspar Ede all this trouble. How very nice! But why should he want to see her again? Did he wish to apologise for his unforgivable conduct?

'I remembered, of course, that you were a clergyman's daughter,' his voice went on, 'and also that you came from Sussex. So I have been traversing this muddy county for the past weeks, seeking small villages, of which there are too many, and enquiring for a Parson Fairweather. It has taken a long time, Grace, but when I discovered Windhaven this afternoon, I realised that my search was over.'

'Did you see my father?' she asked softly.

His lordship placed the grass stem between his teeth and nodded thoughtfully. 'I did, and he was not very polite to me. A stubborn man, your father, once his mind is made up, and with very narrow views on life. Not, I must admit, a fellow after my own heart.'

Grace laughed, a small sound which she tried unsuccessfully to muffle. But she found it impossible to imagine a meeting between her cold, dogmatic father and this handsome, immaculately dressed rake beside her. Whom, she wondered, had come off the better in the battle of wills? She rather hoped that Lord Jaspar was the victor. Not that it really mattered. Neither of them was important to her now, and nothing that either said, or did, could affect her in any way. She was safe, her future and that of her baby was secure, and she was content.

Content, but not happy. Especially after seeing this man again today. He disturbed her with his assurance, his careless, amusing speech and, yes, his admirable looks. She knew that it was disloyal, but she wished that Tom had but a quarter of his lordship's wit, his elegance, and his intelligence.

She could have loved Lord Jaspar,

once, she thought wearily, if he had but stayed that night and sought her affection. But there — he had run off to the Continent, leaving her alone and very upset, and now she had made her plans and would abide by them. It would be pleasant, though, if he would apologise. Did he not realise how greatly he had wronged her?

With a little start of surprise Grace realised that his lordship was still talking.

'Suffice it to say that I learned of your new abode, and of your present condition, in no uncertain terms. Entirely my fault, of course, so here I am to make amends.'

Grace supposed that this was the nearest he would come to an apology; but then lords did not beg pardon; lords were above other mortals; they took what they desired and did not lower themselves to ask permission for their actions.

'You do not speak, Grace?' Lord Jaspar peered at her profile. 'Do you not wish to know what I have in mind?'

She shrugged. It did not matter whether she wished to know, or not. He would tell her anyway. Humility was not a quality which Lord Jaspar Ede would recognise.

'I have decided to let you stay here until the baby is born. It would be too much of an upheaval to move you about the country in your present state. But, once the child is safely delivered and you have recovered your strength, I shall employ a foster mother for the child, and you shall come to London.'

His lordship put out his hand and took hold of hers. She let it lie limply in his warm clasp.

'What say you to that, Grace?' He spoke cheerfully, his plans nicely arranged. 'I shall find a snug little house for you, set you up with a servant, and a cook, and you'll be paid a reasonable sum into the bank each month for your personal use.' Grace tried to remove her hand but his lordship held it tightly. 'Come, Grace, you must answer me.'

'Thank you, sir, for so much consideration, but I must refuse you.'

'You cannot refuse such an offer!' Lord Jaspar let go of her hand and propped himself up on one elbow, leaning forward to see her expression. 'You have no future here. And what of the child? You must consider your baby, Grace?'

'I shall have my baby here and I shall remain in Sussex. I never wish to see London again.' She spoke through tight lips, her anger beginning to mount.

'If you do not want the child fostered, why, then keep it!' his lordship remarked hastily. 'Have it with you in your little house. I do not care. And you'll have money, Grace, for clothes, and furniture, and for anything you may see or desire in the shops.'

Grace turned her head and her great, furious eyes blazed into Lord Jaspar's surprised face. 'I am not a whore, sir! Contrary to what my father believes, and despite the scurrilous way in which you treated me, I am not a whore and will *never* bed with a man for the sake of money!'

She tried to rise but her legs would not hold her.

'Help me up!' she commanded, her face almost as red as her hair.

Slowly his lordship rose to his feet, then he bent and took hold of the girl's arm and lifted her to stand beside him.

'You misunderstand me, dear girl. I wish to set you up as my mistress, that is entirely different to being a common harlot.'

'I know exactly what you mean and am ashamed by your proposition. I am not to be bought, sir!' Grace threw off his supporting hand and took a step away from him. 'I have found a good kind man who has sheltered me these past months, and whom I will marry once the baby is born. If I were not a parson's daughter I would spit on you, sir, for your vile and despicable remarks! Why, you are as bad as Lord Pridmont, and I never thought to meet another man as wicked as him!'

She turned away and began to climb heavily up the hill towards the farmhouse.

Lord Jaspar Ede watched her go, his face an expressionless mask.

* ★ ★ ★

Grace's baby was born on a blustery wet day early in March, it was a girl, and she was named Hope.

Joan had been a great help to Grace. She had shown no pity during the final agonising hours, but she had treated her with rough kindness, giving her a towel to pull on, which she knotted to the bars at the end of Grace's bed.

'Go on, tug at that towel and scream, Miss Grace, scream good and hard whenever you feel it coming. I'll get it out safe and sound, but you've got to do your bit, too.'

Grace had tugged and screamed, and panted and wept, with Joan alternately coaxing and bullying her throughout the painful ordeal. But eventually Hope was born, a strange, red-faced bundle of humanity with a very loud voice.

Once Grace was washed and clad in a clean nightgown, Tom had been allowed into the room and slow, hot tears had slid down Grace's cheeks as she saw the wondering expression on the man's face as he gazed down at the crib beside her.

'Ever so small, ain't she?' he said hoarsely, bending down to touch the baby with one careful finger. 'Never seen one just born before.'

'Hark at the farmer talking!' scoffed Joan, piling up soiled sheets and towels in her arms and making for the door. 'Ain't you never seen newborn calves and lambs then, Tom Laster?'

'Course I have,' he retorted, standing up and staring at her retreating back, 'but this is the first baby child I've seen and it's a wonder.' He shook his head slowly, then looked down at Grace's still form on the bed. 'You all right, Miss Grace? There's no pain, is there?'

'No, Tom.' Grace smiled faintly, her

face whiter than the bolster beneath her head. 'I'm fine, thank you. Just a little tired.'

He nodded. 'You rest easy now and Joan'll bring you up something hot in a while. You must get your strength back so's you can enjoy your little daughter.'

He beamed once more at the tiny mound in the crib and then tiptoed out of the room.

The next morning Sammy was allowed in to see her, and Grace cuddled him beside her with one arm, whilst nursing Hope with her other.

'Oh, Sammy,' she whispered against his golden curls, 'we are a proper family at last, and soon Hope will be bigger and you will be able to play together.' She kissed the top of his head. 'We'll stay in this nice warm house all together and go for walks, and play and sing. Won't that be fun?'

Sammy only understood a part of what she was saying, but he knew that Grace was happy, and he felt secure and greatly loved sitting in the big bed beside her, watching the new, funny pink and white thing which was nuzzling at Grace's breast.

For a fleeting moment Grace thought of Lord Jaspar and wished that he, too, could share in the miracle which they had created between them. But such thoughts were dangerous and Grace put them swiftly from her mind.

How could she ever allow her baby to be given to another woman? And how could she be a good mother and teach her daughter morals and the proper way to behave, if she, herself, were the mistress of a gentleman? Living on his money, yet bearing neither his name, nor taking her proper place in his household?

And he had not mentioned Sammy, she thought indignantly, cuddling the little boy closer to her. Did he, perhaps, envisage finding a foster mother for Sammy also? Or was she supposed to leave him behind with Joan?

Now Grace Fairweather, she told herself firmly before Joan came up to remove the children and settle Grace for her nap, you are never to think of that wretched man again. Rest, and eat, and grow strong, and then have a quiet chat with Tom and get him to decide on a wedding date before Whitsuntide.

★　★　★

One evening, late in April, Grace had settled both children for the night and then gone down to the kitchen. She was waiting for Tom to come in for his evening meal, and for Joan to come downstairs after seeing to the old man.

Grace wore the shabby blue velvet gown in which she had first arrived at the farmhouse, and she regarded her faded skirts with dislike. She could not wear that dreadful garment for much longer and must see if there was another dress amongst the late Mrs Laster's belongings, which could be altered to fit her. Her waist was slowly becoming smaller again, but her breasts were full and heavy with milk, so her velvet bodice gaped alarmingly and would not do up beyond the third button.

Grace sighed, shaking out her long hair and bending forward to let it hang like a curtain before her eyes. She had washed it after putting Sammy to bed, and now dried it in the heat from the range, running her hands through it, liking the feel of the silken tresses as they slipped through her fingers.

If only she could obtain the eight sovereigns which she had brought with her from London. There were any amount of things she could then buy for herself and the children at the market. But the coins were safely hidden away in her bedroom cupboard at the Vicarage, and there was no way to reach them. She would have liked to have bought Tom a present, too. Dear, kind Tom who had given her a home. And Joan, without whom she could never have managed these past months.

As she pondered, the kitchen door opened and Tom strode into the room.

'Ah, Miss Grace, you're all alone, then?' There was an odd expression on his face as he hesitated in the middle of the stone floor, and Grace lifted her head to smile at him, shaking the hair out of her eyes.

'Yes. I do not believe there is anybody here with me,' she mocked gently, 'unless somebody is hiding beneath the table!'

Tom did not smile in return but padded forward to stand before her, a serious expression on his good-natured face.

'Why, Tom, what is the matter?' She stared up at him and saw his eyes fasten on her hair. Grace was suddenly glad that she had washed it that evening, and that it hung free and unbound in a mass of shining bronze upon her shoulders. 'What did you want to say, Tom?' she asked.

Say it now, quickly, whilst we are alone, she thought, trying to smile calmly but seething inwardly with impatience. He was so slow, this man, so kind and patient and lovable, but too ponderous and careful when things of importance needed to be discussed and speedily resolved. And Joan would be down any minute to interrupt them . . .

'Yes, Tom?'

Tom Laster clasped his hands behind his back and shifted his weight from one foot to the other, like some great shambling bear.

'Miss Grace, there is something I have to say to you' He cleared his throat and stared at the floor in front of him.

'Yes?' She sat very still.

'I want to tell you that — er — well, Joan and me, we are to wed, Miss Grace.' His face went very red and he lifted his eyes quickly to glance at her expression.

Grace let out a small moan. It was not possible! It was she, Grace, whom he was to marry. He knew that very well, and so did Joan. Why, Joan was squat and ugly and — and unsuitable.

Swallowing a painful lump in her throat Grace lowered her head, allowing her hair to swing forward concealing her face.

Joan was right for him. Against her will Grace had to admit that. She could work and run about, she was filled with energy and could manage all the things which Grace could not do, not yet.

But Tom had seen her at a disadvantage; at first she had been heavy with child, and now she was still slow-moving and easily tired. In time she, too, would be filled with vigour, and would look after the house even better than Joan. And she was prettier, and possessed a better figure, and she could make Tom laugh!

But a farmer did not need a pretty wife; and Joan was splendid with his father. Grace shivered. She had only seen Mr Laster once, soon after she arrived at the farm, and the sight of him had appalled her. She did not believe that she could care for his bodily needs, feed and wash him, as Joan did. He had lain, open-mouthed and staring-eyed, making strange snuffling noises in his throat, his body rigid under the covers, and his poor, blue-veined hands lying on top of the covers by his sides.

Joan did not make Tom laugh, and they did not speak much together, but they both knew how to work hard, and Tom called her by her first name — there was none of this 'miss' business with her. They were well suited, Grace had to admit that. But was there love between them? Was there even affection, or respect?

'I thought you loved me, Tom?' Grace lifted her head at last and looked up into his worried eyes. 'I thought it would be us.'

'You're too good for me, Miss Grace, you must see that? We don't suit and we'd not get on after a while. You'll want more than I can ever give you. Joan says there was a gentleman in London. Go back to him, Miss Grace, you'll be happier there.'

Grace stared at him. 'Am I to go then? Will you not allow me to stay? For heaven's sake, Tom Laster, speak plainly for once. What do you expect me to do now?'

He cleared his throat. 'We think it'd be best if you went. No hurry, mind. But Joan says two women in the house ain't a good thing. And — and we'd be obliged if you left here when you're ready,' he tailed off miserably.

'I see.' Grace got to her feet, sweeping back her hair in one long jerking movement. 'Well, I'll go, and gladly, Tom Laster. I'll never stay where I'm not made welcome. But I'll need money — I can't get to London, or anywhere else, without a penny to my name. And I'm taking Sammy,' she went on quickly, 'you'll not get rid of me without him. You can tell Joan that, yourself.'

'Yes, Miss Grace, and there ain't no hurry, I tell you. Now don't go flying off in one of your tempers. We'll discuss this nice and easy and make plans — '

'There is nothing to discuss except money.'

'You'll have it.'

'And Sammy — I'll not leave Sammy behind.'

'And Sammy,' he nodded. 'Now stay and have your dinner, Miss Grace, and we'll talk about it good and proper when Joan comes down.'

'I'm not hungry and I do not intend discussing anything with Joan Crump.' She walked to the door and then looked back at the man. 'I'm angry and I'm sad and I'm bitter all at the same time, but I'll never forget your kindness to me, Tom. I won't say this again, but you'll never be forgotten, that's a promise.'

His face crumpled at her words and she flung open the door and hurried away to her room before she, too, disgraced herself and burst into tears.

8

Once again Grace Fairweather sat in the stage coach which was carrying her towards London, but this time she was on her own, with a baby and a small boy for company, whilst Joan remained on the farm with Tom Laster.

Tom had given her money for the journey, and there was enough for several days lodging besides, until she could find herself some work. And Joan had helped her to sew two new dresses from materials which had once belonged to Mrs Laster.

How kind they had both been once they knew that they would soon be rid of her, thought Grace bitterly. Then she sighed and shifted the baby's sleeping weight in her arms. No, that was untrue. Tom had always been kind. It was Joan Crump who had shown a pleasanter side to her nature when she realised that Grace would not remain to compete with her for Tom's attention.

Strangely, the girl had not minded losing Sammy. No doubt Joan would soon be married and producing babies of her own, and once Sammy had been weaned she had begun to lose interest in him, anyway.

No more memories, Grace decided, glancing down at the little boy who lay sleeping quietly against her side, his short legs sticking out before him on the leather seat. Nothing mattered now save to find Mrs Bundle and beg the old dresser to take her in for a while, until she could find lodgings of her own. Lord Jaspar had told her that Mrs Luce no longer lived at the house in Cecil Street, so Mrs Bundle was her only hope.

She would go to the Theatre Royal first, and life would begin from there. How strange it was to be retracing her tracks in little more than a year. Still with Kathy's son in her care, although Grace always thought of him as her own child, and with a baby daughter as well, searching not for Sammy's father but for the stout, kind-hearted woman who had once befriended her.

Grace left her trunk at the inn where she was put down in the Strand, saying that she would send for it in a few hours time. Then she clasped Hope to her bosom, securely wrapped in the folds of her shawl, and took Sammy by the other hand. Very slowly she began to walk through the crowds in the direction of Drury Lane. Sammy's legs would soon tire and she would have to carry him, too, but a little walk would do him good after the confines of the coach.

It was mid-afternoon when Grace paused outside the stage door, thankful to put Sammy down on the steps and give her aching arms a rest. Then she led him up to the door where Ben sat peering out into the hallway.

'What do you want, lady?' he asked, his eyes cross and inquisitive.

'I wish to see Mrs Bundle,' Grace

replied firmly. 'I used to work here. Do you remember me, Ben? I am Grace Fairweather.'

He grunted, surveying her without recognition. So many girls passed in and out of that door, how could he be expected to remember them all?

'Mrs Bundle's gone and children ain't allowed inside,' he muttered.

For a moment Grace swayed against the door post, weariness making the stone floor rock beneath her feet. 'Then can you tell me her address? I must find her before evening and get the babies a bed for the night.'

'She's gone and died,' said Ben with satisfaction. 'You won't be seein' 'er no more.'

'Oh, no!' Grace put her free hand to her head. 'When did she die? How long ago — what ailed her? Whatever shall we do now?'

'Mam!' Sammy sensed her distress and was instantly whimpering, thrusting his face into her skirts, frightened and bewildered at this strange cold place and so many unfamiliar sights and sounds. 'Mam!'

'It's all right, Sammy, dear.' Grace took hold of her emotions and bent to touch the boy's head with a reassuring hand. 'Don't upset yourself — Mama's here and everything is going to be all right.'

But how would it be all right? And where should she go? And who would help her now? It would not be so bad if she were on her own, but with the two little ones she would need food and warmth, and water for washing, and clean beds. As she pondered, Hope began to grizzle at her breast, and Grace knew that she would soon be yelling with hunger.

She thought quickly. 'May I go up to the dressing-room, Ben? There will be no one to disturb at this early hour and I must feed the baby. I cannot think of anywhere else to go just at present, it will give me a breathing space. Please?'

She was tired and depressed and very scared, although she tried not to let her voice tremble in Sammy's hearing. If she could just sit for a while, and tend the baby, she would have time to think.

'Violet's up there.' Ben watched her with his beady eyes. 'All right then, go on up. But don't stay long, mind. I'll be waiting for you.'

Grace smiled gratefully. 'Thank you, Ben.' She bent and took Sammy's hand. 'Come with me, darling, and we'll climb those stairs — see? There are lots of them, and right at the top is a nice room where Mama used to work.'

They plodded slowly upwards, with Hope fretting and squirming with hunger. Then the top landing was reached and Grace knocked on the dressing-room door.

'Come in!' called Violet's voice, and then — 'Lawk's a mercy!' as Grace went in with the two children.

'Well, I never!' Violet Hill stared in amazement as Grace walked to one of the chairs and sat down. Hope was put to her breast, and Sammy was cuddled to her knee with her free hand.

'Whatever are you doin' 'ere, Miss Grace?'

Violet was a thin, mousy female with a long pale face and flat, pale brown hair which she tied in a knot at the back of her head. Grace had never taken much notice of her in the past, and the woman had slid in and out of the dressing-room, unseen and unheard. It was Mrs Bundle who had been Grace's friend and confidant, and although Violet must have helped the other girls, and talked to them, Grace had had nothing to do with her.

'I am glad you remember me,' said Grace, looking across at the woman. 'I was hoping to see Mrs Bundle, but Ben tells me she has died. That was a dreadful shock — I was very fond of her.'

Violet sat with a gown of crimson velvet upon her lap, mending a torn seam. 'Four months ago, it must 'ave bin, she went ever so sudden in the night. Doctor says it were 'er 'eart.'

Grace closed her eyes. It was a lovely way to die, in your sleep like that, but a frightening blow for those who loved you. 'Had she any family?' she asked.

'No.' Violet bit off the thread she was using, then re-threaded her needle with a longer piece of silk. 'Lived all alone, she did. No one to mourn 'er, though some of us went to 'er burial.' She raised her eyes and looked at Sammy with interest. 'You got two now, Miss Grace? What you doin' back in London, then? Country air too much for you, is it?' She grinned, showing blackened teeth, then bent to her sewing once more.

'I am seeking lodgings, Violet,' said Grace slowly, wondering if the woman could help her. 'I need to find somewhere to stay, and then some work. Do you know of any boarding-house, Violet, where I can live with the children? Somewhere clean and not too costly?'

'Fallen on 'ard times, 'ave you? Well, it comes to us all sooner or later.

Where's your 'usband then, Miss Grace? Why don't 'e look after you?'

Grace felt her face grow hot. She did not like being questioned by this female, nor did she care for the knowing look in the other's pale eyes. But she did not dare to answer sharply, she needed Violet's help.

'I haven't got a husband,' she said softly, bending forward and laying a kiss on Hope's downy head. This little girl would not suffer for lack of a father, nor would Sammy, she would make sure of that, and would fight for them both with every breath within her body. 'I am on my own, but I can work and I *shall* find work.' Grace lifted her head and looked fiercely at her companion. 'But first I must find somewhere to stay. Can you help me find a place?'

Violet stood up and shook out the scarlet gown, then she walked over to the cupboard and hung the gown carefully away.

'You can come 'ome with me,' she said. 'It's only one room but it's comfy, like, and you're welcome for a day or two till you've sorted yourself out.'

'Oh, I'd be so grateful!' Grace stared at the woman's angular figure, relief shining from her face. 'And I can pay you, Violet, I have some money with me.' Suddenly words flowed from her as hope surged through her body. 'What play is on at the moment? Are they looking for understudies? Have you seen anything of Mr Mellish? I could act again if there was a chance of a part.'

'Play's bin running a fortnight but it's not a success — reckon it'll be taken off soon. Haven't seen nothing of Mr Mellish, but they're wanting a cleaner out front, I do believe. You'd best make enquiries in the morning, miss.'

'I will,' said Grace quickly. 'I do not mind what I do so long as I earn a little money for the three of us.'

'But what'll you do about the babe?' Violet's eyes strayed to Hope at her mother's breast. 'You'll 'ave to find a wet-nurse — can't go working with a

219

babe, and all.' She looked again at Sammy, who clung to Grace's skirts, his thumb in his mouth. 'You is in a pickle, Miss Grace, that's for sure. Who's the father of these two, then?'

Grace sighed. 'It's a long and complicated story and not one I'm telling you now. But I'd be grateful for a room, Violet, and I'll call here tomorrow about that cleaning job. Then, if I get it, I shall have to find a wet-nurse. But it must be someone kind.' She looked up with a grim expression on her face. 'I'm not leaving my babies with anyone I do not trust.'

'My cousin's lately 'ad a little boy, plenty of milk, she 'as, maybe she'll be willing to assist you.' Violet smiled across at Sammy. 'What's your name, sonny? Let's see if Violet's got something nice for you, shall we?' She fumbled in the pocket of her apron and drew out a small paper package. 'It's for me tea but I reckon it can be shared with you.' She sat down again and unwrapped the paper. Inside was a squashed sticky bun. Carefully, Violet broke it in two pieces and held out one half to the little boy. ''Ere you are, you 'ave a munch on that, sonny.'

Sammy looked up at Grace who smiled and gave a nod. 'Go on, you may take it, Sammy.' She gave him a push in Violet's direction. 'His name is Sammy and he's sixteen months old.'

'Beautiful boy, not a bit like you, Miss Grace, with that lovely golden 'air and big blue eyes. Who's 'is pa, then?'

Grace wished that the woman were not so curious, but she supposed that such interest was natural. Here she was, arriving from nowhere, with ringless hands and two babies under the age of two. Of course it was puzzling, but she did not intend baring her soul to anyone just yet.

'I will tell you the whole story one day,' she said lightly, lifting Hope against her shoulder and rubbing her back. 'Now, when you have time I should like to go to your room. Will you give me instructions as to how to find it, or can you take me there?'

'Going there meself,' said Violet, standing up and brushing the crumbs from her lap. 'There's time enough before the girls come in, and it's not far from 'ere — just behind the market in King Street.'

Violet's room was warm and cosy, and quite well furnished. Grace was surprised that a woman in Violet's position should be able to afford what amounted to moderate luxury. There was a small range which was burning brightly; a far corner had been curtained off and behind this Grace was shown a washing area complete with ewer and basin, and a clean white towel.

'You can wash the children there,' said Violet, 'I'll put a pan of water on to heat this very minute.'

A feather bed stood against one wall, and a dresser and a cupboard stood against the other wall. There was a table in the middle of the room with three stools tucked away beneath it; red curtains hung at the window, and a gay rug made of different coloured rags lay upon the floorboards.

Violet's room was on the ground floor, off the hallway, and at the other end of the hall was a back door which led out to the yard.

'Two privies out there,' remarked Violet with satisfaction, 'an' a pump just round the corner for water. What you think of my place, then, Miss Grace?'

'It's very nice,' said Grace truthfully. Indeed, it was far better than she could have hoped for.

'You and me and Sammy can tuck ourselves into that bed, it's good and wide, and I'll empty a drawer and make a bed for the baby in no time.'

Suddenly the woman was busy, running here and there about the room, putting a pan of water to heat upon the range, pulling out linen from one of the drawers, placing the empty drawer beside the bed and then laying towels in the bottom of it, to make a snug resting place for Hope.

'Oh,' said Grace, 'I've forgotten all about my trunk. I said I would fetch it from the inn as soon as I'd found somewhere to live.'

'Then you go there now and I'll look after the little ones,' said Violet helpfully. 'If you go quickly, miss, you'll have time to get there and back before I have to leave for the theatre.'

The following morning Violet again took charge of the children, and Grace went to enquire about the cleaning job at the Lane. But to her dismay she was told that the vacancy had been filled, and they were not requiring any more cleaners for the time being. She returned to King Street in a perturbed state of mind.

'I shall just have to go on looking,' she said, as they sat down to a mid-day meal of mutton and potatoes. 'Maybe, when the new play is cast, I shall be able to get a part. Please tell me when this present production finishes.'

Violet nodded. 'But it won't be for a couple of weeks yet,' she said. 'Why don't you tell me everything?' she went on, her light eyes watching the girl's despondent face. 'We've got time this afternoon, and I reckon I can 'elp you better when I knows the full story.'

'Haven't you helped me enough as it is?' said Grace wearily. 'Dear heavens, if only I could stand on my own two feet! How very satisfying that would be. But I seem incapable of managing on my own.'

'Come on now,' said Violet cheerfully, 'do you good to get things off your chest. Sammy's that weary and can 'ave a lay down on the bed, then you can tell me all about yourself.'

Whilst Sammy and Hope slept, Grace perched herself on one of the stools, with Violet sitting opposite her at the table, and told her companion all about Katharine Lang, and her search for Lord P.

'I expect you knew my friend in the old days,' said Grace. 'She was at the Lane for a while, using the name of Kaye Fair.'

Violet's hands fell to her knees and two spots of colour appeared on her pale face. 'Well now, fancy that! I never 'eard you speak of 'er before — 'course I knowed 'er!'

'I told Mrs Bundle,' Grace said, surprised by the other's excitement. 'I used to stay later, if you remember, after you and the other girls had left for the night, and we used to chat then. I do wish she was still alive,' she added wistfully, 'I should so like to see her again.'

'Now don't you go getting miserable with me,' said Violet sharply, 'and I got news for *you*. Why didn't you never ask me about Kaye Fair?'

'You knew her well?' When Mrs Bundle had told her about Kathy, Grace had not thought to question anyone else. And Violet had always been a shadowy, rather insignificant person, tending to the other girls and then leaving the theatre quickly once her tasks were done. 'What did you know of Kathy? Do you think Lord Pridmont

226

was Sammy's father? What happened to Kathy after she left the theatre and before she returned home? Mrs Bundle said she never heard from her again.'

'She come 'ere.' Violet nodded in satisfaction at the expression on Grace's face. 'When she got too fat to go on with 'er acting I gives 'er a place 'ere and she stayed till she 'ad Sammy.'

'But why didn't she let Mrs Bundle know? She was so worried about her.'

''Cos she didn't want no nagging and grumbling. Mrs B were always on at 'er, never leaving poor Kaye alone, and she were fed up with it.' Violet gazed across at the bed where Sammy lay sleeping. 'Fancy that! I never knowed it were the very same child wot I 'elped into the world. Well, I never!'

'Why did Kathy leave you? Why did she come back to Windhaven when she was so sick? The journey almost killed her and she never recovered from it.'

'She weren't right after the birth.' Violet looked past Grace with unseeing, contemplative eyes. 'Something wrong with 'er innards, there was. The doctor, 'e weren't 'appy about 'er at all. But Kaye, she wants to go 'ome to see her old Gran, and one day she ups and goes and I don't see 'er no more.'

'Poor Kathy.' Grace dropped her head forward on her chest. Poor sick, lonely Kathy, making that long journey home to Windhaven in pain and anguish, knowing that she was soon to die. 'It was Lord Pridmont, wasn't it?' Grace raised her head with a jerk, her voice filled with anger. 'He was the father, wasn't he?'

Violet nodded, biting her lip.

'Then why didn't he help her? Why didn't he give her money? He has enough for himself with that fine house, and all those servants and beautiful possessions. Why didn't he do something for her and the baby?'

'She wouldn't take nothing,' said Violet. ''E's always good to 'is young ladies afterwards, like, but Kaye wouldn't 'ave nothing more to do with 'im. Silly, I thought, but that was 'er way and she was determined to suffer.'

Something in the tone of her voice alerted Grace. 'Did *you* know Lord Pridmont, Violet?' she asked.

Violet stared back at the girl, her head high. 'Yes,' she said stonily. 'I were beautiful once, and 'e wanted me and paid me right well. That's 'ow I got this room and all these nice things, *and* money in the bank. I bin careful these past years, Miss Grace, and 'e give me a real good start in life.'

Another of his young ladies! What a dreadful man he was. Mrs Bundle had been right, and she, Grace, should never have had anything to do with him.

'You were fortunate,' said Grace softly, 'because you did not have a baby. I can understand how Kathy must have felt when he refused to marry her. Oh, men are beasts! I'm *glad* she did not accept any money from him. That would have been an immoral thing to do.' She stood up and began to pace the room, thinking suddenly of Lord

Jaspar, and his offer of help. 'Men always think that money makes up for any crime and any evil deed. How despicable they are. And Lord Pridmont would not marry her — great ugly toad — because he thought himself too good for my friend. My Kathy!' She spun round on Violet. 'My sweet, kind, goodnatured friend, who was worth ten times that odious and unhealthy aristocrat!'

'Well, I'd rather be comfortable and accept payment that's me due, than be proud and starving,' announced Violet. 'And look at you, miss, what 'appened to you? Refused payment, I suppose? All 'igh and mighty, I suppose? And now you're begging from me, and from anyone else wot's better off than you are.'

'How dare you!' Grace cried. 'How dare you speak to me like that! You may be a whore and enjoy receiving money from evil old men, but I shall *never* be bribed!'

'Was you like Kaye, then?' asked

Violet, in no way perturbed by Grace's fury. 'Did you refuse Lord Pridmont's money and allow pride to uphold you? Well, I'm sorry for you and sorry for those little ones. I reckon you're a selfish girl, Miss Grace, 'scuse me for saying so, but you've two little ones to think of now, and how you going to feed and clothe them? Pride is all very well but it don't provide bread nor garments.'

'Don't you preach at me, Violet Hill! I've had enough of that all my life.' Grace was red with passion and she stormed up and down the room, clutching at her skirts with trembling hands. 'And it was not Lord Pridmont. I would not have allowed him to touch me with a barge pole!'

'Ho, ho!' said Violet with glee. 'Who's bin a naughty girl, then? You're not so virtuous as you make out, dearie. I seen you going off with that Richard Mercury and you bin to Lord Pridmont's 'ouse more than once — so who's calling who a whore then? At least I stuck to one gentleman. Which one's the father of little Hope, or don't you know?'

'You hush your mouth, Violet Hill! And I'll be leaving here at the first possible moment. I'll not take any more insults from you!' Grace shook her fist in the woman's face, almost knocking her off her stool. 'Don't you ever talk like that to me again!'

''Ow much money 'ave you got left, then?' Violet laughed into Grace's enraged face. 'You leave 'ere and then where are you going? It'll be into the streets with you, my fair lady, and you'll be any man's then, just for the asking. Oh, I seen girls desperate before, and you won't be the last of 'em. Can't manage without money, Miss Grace, and that's a fact. Wot you ain't realised is that everything I 'ave 'ere, and all the comforts wot I've shared with you, 'ave bin provided by Lord Pridmont. What about that then? It don't matter to you because I've earned 'em, I suppose? And you've not dirtied your white body, is that it? But you're a hippycrit, miss, and your precious friend Kathy were the same. You takes all you can from others, but don't try to provide for yourselves.'

Grace felt for her stool with one hand and pulled it beneath her shaky legs. Her face was pale and shiny with sweat.

'Let's talk this over quietly,' she said, her voice hoarse with emotion. 'We have been shrieking at each other like a couple of fishwives and it is not the way to be discussing the future at all.'

'Very well,' answered Violet, folding her hands upon her lap and staring across at Grace with triumphant eyes. 'So, what's your plan, then?'

Grace swallowed. 'I shall go out tomorrow and visit other theatres in this district, and see if they are requiring people for walk-on parts, or cleaners, or any kind of assistants. I have had some theatrical experience, so that might help. I *am* grateful for what you are doing for us, Violet, believe me, and I intend paying my way so that you will not be out of pocket. But I shall have to find work first.'

'As you like.' Violet shrugged and slid off her stool. 'I'd best get ready to go out now. But you think it over, miss. If a gentleman's prepared to look after you and pay you regular money, it's a chance not to be missed, I reckon. Pity of it were me looks went early on and that Lord P soon tired of me. Same with Kaye — she got fat and miserable, and 'e don't like that. But you — ' she turned and looked over her shoulder at Grace, 'you've still got a pretty face and figure, and you ought to make the most of 'em whilst they last.'

'Thank you, Violet,' said Grace quietly, 'I shall think over what you've said.'

Once the woman had gone and Grace was left on her own, she did ponder over Violet's words. But it was not of Lord Pridmont that she thought — wicked man, she could never contemplate being loved by him. Nor did she consider Richard Mercury.

Having not seen that golden young man for almost a year, his charm and remarkable good looks had faded from her mind. The man she thought about was Lord Jaspar Ede; the man who had seduced her; who had fathered her adorable daughter, and who, moreover, she knew she could very easily love.

Lord Jaspar had wanted her, he had sought her all over Sussex, and he had seen her large and unattractive, and shabbily dressed, yet had *still* made his offer.

And yet . . . the teachings of her father were etched into her mind, engrained, as it were, into her very skin. How could she forget, or ignore, his standards? And the morals, the rigid views with which she had grown up? Ever since she was a little girl, Grace had dreamed of being happily married, of keeping house for a kind and loving husband, of growing old with him and watching their offspring mature and flourish.

And what would her children think of

their mother when they grew up? How could they be proud of her, or respect her, or even love her, if she were but a common trollop? And what sort of a standard would she be setting them? How could they grow into strong and healthy and pure-minded adults if her shocking conduct was ever before their innocent eyes?

Grace let out a small moan, rocking her body from side to side, not knowing what decision to make, beset by problems which she could not solve.

Then Hope stirred in her makeshift bed and began to whimper.

Hope. Grace was glad that she had named her daughter that. She walked across to lift the baby into her arms, and for a moment peace filled her heart and she found comfort in suckling the little girl.

Tomorrow, Grace thought, sitting down on the bed and smiling at Sammy who was also wakening from his nap, tomorrow everything would be all right. A job would be found, and then somewhere of their own where they could live quietly and happily together.

She smiled and bent her head to kiss the baby's hair.

★ ★ ★

The next morning, feeling light of heart and certain of success, Grace left the children in Violet's care and walked the streets around the Strand, visiting the Lyceum, and the Theatre Royal, Covent Garden; the Haymarket, and various other smaller, private theatres which were tucked away down side streets and alleys. But always the answer was the same. There were no vacancies, and nobody required her services.

Eventually, Grace wandered as far as Bedford Square and with a strange feeling of recognition, she walked along the pavement until she came to No 17. This was the home of Lord Jaspar Ede. Grace passed it quickly in case he should be peering out of one of the windows, and then she paused and looked back at the building.

For a long moment she studied the façade — the shiny, black-painted door and railings, the white steps, and the highly-polished brass doorknocker. But this would never be her home. She and the children would be ensconced in a little house in a less-prosperous corner of town; they would be hidden away from his lordship's family and friends, never acknowledged publicly, visited only when Lord Jaspar felt so inclined.

Grace gave her head a little shake and began walking hurriedly back in the direction from which she had come. That was not the answer. She would have to wait for the present play to finish, and then apply for a part in the new production at Drury Lane. If she lived very frugally for the next few weeks, her remaining pence might just last until then.

She was panting as she opened the door into the hallway of Violet's lodging house, and she could hear Hope screaming as she sped across the hall.

She was late and the baby was starving. Poor Violet. Grace hoped that the woman had not been worried by her lengthy absence.

Grace opened the door to their room and then stopped abruptly. Neither Violet nor Sammy were there. She crossed the room, her forehead puckering in a frown as she lifted the hysterical baby into her arms.

'Hush, now, my sweeting, Mammy's home.'

She sat herself down on the bed and wondered where the other two had disappeared to, as Hope subsided into silence at her breast. Had they gone for a walk? Had Violet gone to the market, or to the shops? Perhaps they were only in the back yard?

Grace did not worry unduly until the baby had been fed and changed and put back into her drawer, where she gurgled softly to herself. There was still no sign of the woman and the small boy, so Grace went out into the passage and through the back door to the yard.

There was nobody in the privies and the yard was deserted.

As she came back into the house, the front door opened and, silhouetted from the light outside, Grace could see the figure of Violet Hill accompanied by a man. She ran towards them, her heart beating in terror. Had there been an accident? Was he a doctor?

'Where's Sammy?' she cried, in a thin, high voice. 'What has happened to him?'

'It's all right, miss.' Violet's words were crisply confident. 'Sammy's all right and this gentleman wants to see you.'

They came further into the hall and Grace looked into the smiling eyes of Richard Mercury.

'You!' she whispered, her hands going to her bosom, trying to still the agitated beating of her heart. 'What do you want? And where is Sammy?'

'Come along in,' said Violet, pushing her way past them, 'we can't talk in the 'all.'

Mercury took Grace's arm and led her into the room. 'Sit down, Miss Grace,' he said, in his soft, caressing voice, 'and calm yourself. All is well, so do not be alarmed.'

Grace sat bolt upright on one of the stools, and Violet and Richard Mercury seated themselves on the other stools around the table.

'See 'ere, miss, Mister Mercury's got wot's called a proppysition to make and it'll solve all your problems, see if it don't.' She nodded her head and then removed her bonnet.

'Miss Grace.' Mercury leaned forward, resting his elbows upon the table, his vivid blue eyes gazing at her with compassion and admiration. 'Violet has been telling us of your predicament and Lord Pridmont would like to help you.'

'Oh, how could you!' Grace turned her head and glared at the older woman. 'How could you do such a thing? And what have you done with Sammy?'

'He is safely with us, Miss Grace, in a beautiful room and with his own servants to look after him. He will want for nothing, I do assure you.' Mercury stretched out a hand and covered her clenched fist. 'That is the answer, my dear. You are to come to Cavendish Square to live with us, your children, too, and Lord Pridmont will make himself responsible for all of you. I cannot think of a better solution and, indeed, am awed all over again by his lordship's kindness to those less fortunate than himself.'

Grace remembered the ugly fat body, and the white puffed skin; his tiny evil eyes and slobbery lips.

'Never, never, never!' she whispered, shuddering. 'I want Sammy brought back now, do you hear? And I'll not accept one penny from Lord Pridmont. *Nothing*, I tell you!'

'Then I fear that you'll not see Sammy again,' replied Mercury, sitting back and folding his arms upon his chest. 'You will not see the boy again unless you come with me and accept his lordship's offer of help.'

9

For a long moment Grace stared across at the beautiful young man whom she had once so admired. She knew now that he was dangerous and not to be trusted. She had also sworn never to see Lord Pridmont again. But Sammy! The little boy was her own son now; she could not abandon him to that house of wickedness and sin.

She would have to pretend; would have to go along with their plans; be docile and admiring and look for a chance to escape when the time was right.

'I'll not be parted from Hope.' She stared into Mercury's brilliant blue eyes.

'I am sure that Lord Pridmont will give you all a home,' answered Richard Mercury softly. 'He has forgiven you for your foolish behaviour last time you left us, and is willing to give you a second chance.'

How could she ever escape him again? Grace lowered her eyes to disguise the feverish motions of her brain, which twisted this way and that like a rat in a cage. Once she was within his clutches he would make certain not to lose her a second time. And she could not bear him. Never would she allow him to touch her again!

She lifted her head and gazed across the table at Violet, who sat opposite her so calmly, so complacently, watching Grace with a cruel, satisfied smile upon her thin lips.

How much had she been paid for her information, thought Grace? What price had been paid for the small, golden-haired son of that lecherous beast? And if they went to live there, how long would it be before the boy began to ape his father's vile ways? No child should be forced to grow up in that household; no innocent should be corrupted by that evil old man. She could not go there — she could not!

Grace slid off her stool, biting her lip. There was a choice. A choice of two evils, yes, but one was far greater than the other. Lord Jaspar Ede desired her. He was also a lord and a wealthy man and, with him, she and the children would be safe. And she would far, far rather lie in his bed than in that of the fat toad Pridmont. She still had a choice — if Lord Jaspar could be found.

'Are you coming, Miss Grace?' Mercury had risen from the table and was standing beside her. 'Lord Pridmont is awaiting your decision and wishes to see you himself.'

'I am coming.' Grace looked quickly around the room. Hope had been fed and would lie quietly for some time. Was Violet to be trusted with her? It seemed likely that the woman had done her worst and with Grace in the company of Lord Pridmont and Richard Mercury, Grace did not believe that Violet would dare to hurt the baby. And

Grace needed to leave Hope behind. It suited her purpose to have some reason for returning to King Street that night.

'I shall come with you now and see Lord Pridmont,' she said to Richard Mercury, 'and also see for myself that Sammy is all right.' She reached for her shawl and flung it around her shoulders.

'Good.' Mercury took her arm and guided her towards the door. 'We will go at once before you change your mind.'

'What about the baby?' Violet called after them.

'I'll be back for her,' Grace said over her shoulder. 'I must see Sammy and arrange things, then I'll return for Hope and my belongings.'

'We'll send for them,' said Mercury, 'come along now, Miss Grace, I've wasted enough time as it is and his lordship will be getting impatient.' He opened the door and Grace was accompanied across the hall and down the front steps to the waiting carriage.

'You are very quiet,' he remarked, as they began to jolt on their way. 'Of what are you thinking?'

Grace summoned up all her strength. 'I am thinking of the future,' she said quietly. 'Thinking of the children, and of myself, and realising that this is probably the best solution for us all.'

Would he believe her? It was vital that both he and Lord Pridmont should trust her change of heart.

Mercury nodded. 'I hope that you are truly grateful,' he said. 'I hope that you realise what it is to be singled out like this by his lordship, for his special attention. No other female has ever scorned his affection and then been forgiven.'

Grace forced a smile to her dry lips. 'When I was last at Cavendish Square I was a foolish and empty-headed young girl. Since then, life has not been kind to me and I have learned many a hard lesson. This time, I believe, Lord Pridmont will find me both appreciative of his attention and docile towards his demands.'

The coach drew to a halt outside the large white mansion and Mercury helped her to alight. Once again Grace was ushered into the magnificent hall of Lord Pridmont's residence, but this time she was neither awed nor intimidated by such grandeur.

God help me to act well, she thought grimly, as Mercury escorted her up the red-carpeted stairway. More than one life would depend on her ability to deceive this afternoon.

Lord Pridmont lay reclining in the huge, plant-filled room where Grace had first seen him. There was no music today and the screen at the far end of the room had been folded back. Pridmont gazed at her intently with his tiny black eyes as she moved slowly towards him. He was wearing a long, loose robe of rose pink, an incongruous colour on his fat male form, and his bald head was covered by a pink turban.

'As beautiful as ever, I see,' he said in his soft, breathy voice, 'but oh, dearie me, what have you got on, dear girl?

That gown is a travesty! Rich, how can you present her to me in such abominable attire?'

'I beg your pardon, sir, but Miss Grace was in a great hurry to see you and I was not certain if she possessed another gown.'

Lord Pridmont sniggered and popped a jellied fruit into his mouth. 'Not finding life quite so pleasant these days, I hear? Well, well, perhaps we can remedy that. Sit down, sit down, do not stand over me, I beg. And cover yourself with that.' He flung a silken robe in Grace's direction.

It was a light, embroidered garment of deep blue silk, with birds sewn upon it in turquoise and pink and grey threads. Grace sank down upon a pile of cushions and covered herself with the robe as best she could. Mercury squatted beside her as Lord Pridmont went on speaking.

'Rich has told you of what I propose? You are willing to come here and live with me?'

Grace nodded. 'If I may have the children here also.'

Pridmont eyed her carefully, his small mouth sucking at the sweet 'The boy remains, of course, I have decided to lay claim to him. As for the other — what is it, a boy or girl!'

'A little girl.' Grace held her hands tightly together.

'A little girl,' Pridmont repeated, and beamed. 'I like little girls. Is she pretty?'

'I do not know yet — she is only two months old.'

If she could not escape, if she and Sammy and Hope were doomed to stay here forever, what would become of Hope?

'Good, good, we'll take her, won't we, Rich?' Pridmont chuckled his fat chuckle. 'Now, you understand that you are to live here, as my wife, have beautiful clothes and — '

'Your wife?' Grace gasped, not believing what she heard.

'Of course.' Lord Pridmont turned and searched with his plump fingers for another sweet from the silver dish beside him. 'I want it lawful and final. You see, I do not trust you, my dear, and cannot have you running off with Ede, or any other gentleman when it pleases you to do so.' He swung his head round and stared at her, his expression hardening. 'You have vexed me considerably, Miss Grace, and I'll not tolerate such behaviour a second time. As my wife you will have to obey me totally and I shall, of course, have complete control over you.

'It is a very great honour which I bestow upon you, but I have been thinking for some time that it would be pleasant to have a female permanently here, to order my household, and to play hostess on the necessary occasions. You are fair of face and figure, I like the idea of wedding with a parson's daughter, and you are young enough to please me for many years to come. I believe you will do quite nicely, yes, indeed.'

'His lordship is most kind,' muttered

Richard Mercury, frowning at Grace and nodding at her to say something.

'Most kind,' she whispered faintly.

'As you found my appearance somewhat ill-pleasing last time we met and had the audacity to show your repugnance, we will now let you in on a little secret.' Lord Pridmont smiled, his good humour restored. 'To set your mind at rest, Miss Grace, I wish to assure you that I shall not carry out the normal duties of a man to his wife. That is to say, I shall not be an actual husband to you. I am somewhat overweight, and my age is also against me. I like only to touch and to watch. Fortunately, Rich here is more than willing to perform for me, so I do not think that you will find our union too unpleasant.' He laughed thickly. 'Eh, Rich, you'll enjoy the sport with the lovely Miss Grace, will you not? Or should I say — Lady Pridmont?'

'I shall indeed, sir.' Mercury smiled and then turned his eyes upon Grace, who sat rigid beside him.

She was revolted by what she had just heard but one fact was suddenly clear. Sammy was not the son of Lord Pridmont, he was Richard Mercury's offspring. Kathy, too, had been ensnared in this trap. And Violet? No wonder she had been so curious about Sammy's father — his fair hair and bright blue eyes must have alerted her.

Why, oh, why had she, Grace, not heeded Mrs Bundle's advice and refused to have anything to do with Lord Pridmont and his handsome young messenger? Lord Jaspar had warned her as well but she had taken no notice of his words. Now she was caught as firmly as a fly in a spider's web. And to think that she would be expected to lie in Richard Mercury's arms, to allow him to make love to her *in the presence of Lord Pridmont*!

Grace kept her head lowered, terrified lest her feelings become apparent to the two men. How could anyone act in such bestial fashion? Poor Kathy had presumably been used in such a way and had finally paid for her sins by subsequent sickness and then death. What vile and inhuman monsters these two were!

Grace lifted her head and glanced swiftly at the young man beside her. Lord Pridmont had always revolted her so she was not surprised by anything he said or did. But she had thought Richard Mercury to be a better man. Indeed, she had once believed herself to be in love with him. Now she looked at his beautiful face and saw for the first time the weak, almost girlish droop to his lips, and the round softness of his chin. But his eyes, as they stared at her, were like a china doll's; hard, round and expressionless.

Grace curved her own mouth into a smile as she caught Mercury's gaze upon her. Miss Kelly had once taught her to act; now she must display her talent as never before.

'I shall be charmed by Mr Mercury's company,' she murmured, lowering her lashes and pouting demurely. 'I am also honoured by your lordship's proposal of marriage and pray that I prove worthy of such a great compliment.'

'You will, my dear, you will. Do not forget that I control every person in this house and if you disobey me, or even displease me, Miss Grace, it will be your children who will be made to suffer.'

Grace bowed her head in submission, and said softly,

'May I have leave to return to King Street this afternoon and collect Hope, sir? I also have a few belongings which I must gather together. Then I am yours, to do with as you will. I could never allow my children to suffer for my folly.'

'Well said, young lady,' answered Pridmont, 'I believe we shall get along very well together. Now, let us begin as we mean to go on. You come here and live with us and I shall carry out my side of the bargain and engage a parson to wed us in proper fashion.

'Rich, go with her now, she has not entirely convinced me that she is to be trusted, and bring her safely back with her belongings. This will be a night to remember. Oh, gracious me, yes!'

He laughed and licked at his sticky fingers. 'Then see Abigail, Rich, and arrange for Miss Grace to be dressed in more becoming apparel. I cannot abide the sight of my future bride as she is at present.'

'I shall see to everything, sir.' Mercury stood up and held out his hand to Grace. 'Come,' he said, 'let us return to King Street and finish your business there, at once.'

'May I see Sammy before I go?' Grace rose and looked down at her husband-to-be. 'I should like to make sure that he is not frightened in such unfamiliar surroundings.'

'The boy is fine, I can assure you of that, and no, I think you must wait until your return, Miss Grace.' Pridmont stared up at her through narrowed eyes. 'Go now, quickly, and you may see the boy when you come back.'

Grace turned without a word and

followed Richard Mercury from the room. Her heart was heavy, but she realised that she would have to put Sammy to the back of her mind for the moment. What mattered now was the outwitting of her companion. If her plan failed, then both she and the babies were doomed.

They seated themselves in the carriage and were once again on their way.

'You know,' remarked Grace, willing her voice to sound calm, 'it was only when Lord Pridmont mentioned you that I knew marriage with him would be possible. I could not have borne to have been his wife in the full sense of the word.' She gave a delicate shudder. 'But you, sir,' the dimple appeared in her cheek, 'why, you stole my heart that very first night at the Lane when you came to the dressing-room and invited me to dine with his lordship. Do you remember?'

'I do indeed.' Mercury sounded amused. 'You were wearing that black taffeta gown from the Ballroom scene and looked quite ravishing, if my memory serves me right.'

'I thought *you* were the most handsome man I had ever seen in my life,' said Grace truthfully.

'But since then you have been wooed by Lord Jaspar Ede.' Mercury shifted on the seat and his voice was cold. 'Tell me, Miss Grace, why did you not turn to him for help? He is the father of your baby, is he not?'

'Yes,' answered Grace, 'but he took advantage of my innocence, he took me against my will, and I shall never forgive his selfish and brutal behaviour. He is a cruel man, sir, and although he asked me to become his mistress I could *never* contemplate such a relationship! Besides,' she softened her tone, 'I always hoped that by coming to London I might see you again, Mr Mercury.'

She saw Mercury smile in the semi-darkness of the swaying carriage and she relaxed. She was but one of the many females who had been bewitched by his striking looks, he had no reason not to believe her.

'I think we shall get on very well, you and I,' he said, 'and hopefully, you will be more sensible than other young ladies of my experience. Your friend, Kaye Fair, was a foolish young woman, but then she expected more than we were prepared to give.'

'I suppose she wanted you to marry her once she knew that she was carrying your child?'

'Something like that,' he retorted curtly. 'But no promises had been made as I never intend marrying, and Lord Pridmont did not consider her the right sort of female to satisfy his very particular nature. She had only herself to blame for the outcome, silly chit!'

Grace felt her anger mount at the scornful way in which the young man spoke about her beloved friend. But she breathed deeply, as Miss Kelly had taught her, to master self-control, and held her hands tightly on her lap.

'Then I am indeed fortunate,' she

managed to answer sweetly, 'that Lord Pridmont wishes to make me his wife, and that you will always be near to support me.'

The carriage drew to a halt outside Violet's lodgings and Grace sat forward.

'Will you wait for me, sir? I shall not be more than a couple of minutes, having so few belongings, and will take but a moment to gather them together and to wrap Hope in her blanket.'

'Very well.' Mercury opened the door for her and assisted her down onto the pavement. 'I do not greatly care for Violet Hill, I must confess, and will wait out here in the street for you. But hurry, Miss Grace, for his lordship is an impatient man.'

Grace flashed him a radiant smile and then scuttled into the house. She opened the door to Violet's room and saw the woman busy at the range, stirring a pan of soup.

'Dear Violet,' Grace cried, 'I cannot thank you enough for what you have done! Lord Pridmont has asked me to marry him, and I shall soon be a *real* lady, just imagine that!'

Envy and annoyance flickered across Violet's face as she heard the news, then she turned back to the fire. 'Nice for you, I'm sure.'

'And I'm going to have new gowns, scores of them, and jewels and petti-coats and shoes and shawls! He's going to allow me to have both children with me and oh, we are going to have a splendid time!'

As she was speaking, Grace swooped about the room picking up objects, gathering together her meagre posses-sions, pulling out the tin trunk from beneath the bed and flinging everything into it. Then she bent over the drawer and lifted out her sleeping daughter.

'There — that is everything, I think. I shall send for my trunk in the morning, Violet, if you will allow it to stay here until then. Now I'm off to the privy, and then Richard Mercury is taking us to our new home. Good luck and goodbye, Violet, thank you for allowing us to stay with you.'

Grace clasped Hope to her bosom with one hand and raised the other in a wave, smiling at the woman's dour expression. Then she opened the door and let herself out into the hall. Securing Hope firmly in the folds of her shawl, she fled down the hall to the back door and let herself out into the yard. From there, a narrow passage led out into the street.

Grace did not run for fear of drawing attention to herself, but she walked as fast as she dared, thankful that there were plenty of people about and hoping that she would remain unnoticed amongst the crowds. She had to get to Bedford Square, and she had to see Lord Jaspar Ede. Only he could help her now.

Fiercely Grace clutched the baby to her breast as her feet sped along the street. Hope would soon be safe, but what of Sammy? She must get help at once and persuade Lord Jaspar to go and rescue the boy from Lord Pridmont's residence. Grace dreaded the thought of the fat man's anger, and knew that he would not hesitate to harm the child in order to punish her for her defiance.

How long would Mercury wait for her to appear from Violet's house? Would he go straight back to Cavendish Square with the news of her flight? Or would he spend time in trying to find her? And what if Lord Jaspar were not at home? What would she do then?

Biting her lip, she strode onwards, her head erect and her eyes straining ahead in fearful anxiety. Grace did not see the pallid faces of the passers-by; she saw only Sammy's little stricken face. He would be so lonely, so bewildered without his Mam to comfort him.

She also saw the sagging, pale face of Lord Pridmont in her mind's eye; and his rose-bud mouth, folded tightly away in fury when he heard of her escape from Richard Mercury.

Casting a swift look behind her, Grace saw that the road was clear, then she turned the corner into Bedford Square. She almost ran for the last few yards and bounded up the steps of No 17, breathless and trembling with fatigue.

The door swung open to her knock and she saw the grave-faced butler standing before her. No emotion showed on his impassive countenance as he studied her worn gown, her bare head, and the baby bundled up in her shawl.

'Yes, miss?' enquired Carlton politely.

'Is Lord Jaspar at home? And may I come in and wait for him if he is not here?' she said quickly. 'I need sanctuary, Carlton, and must not be seen waiting out in the street.'

The butler swung the door wide open and bowed. 'Take a seat, if you please, miss. I shall enquire if his lordship is at home. What name shall I give?'

Grace sank down thankfully on the carved wooden bench in the hall and watched the front door shut firmly behind the butler's rigid back. 'Tell him it is Grace Fairweather, and please say it is *most* urgent.'

Carlton trod purposefully away down the hallway and mounted the stairs to the first floor. Grace sat rocking the baby and waited. She and Hope were both safe — now it was Sammy who mattered.

At last the butler appeared again, standing on the landing at the top of the first flight of stairs. He coughed to attract her attention. 'His lordship will see you now. Please come up, Miss Fairweather.'

Grace climbed the stairs and then followed the butler's retreating back past the dining-room, which she remembered from her earlier visits, and on to a room opposite which proved to be a smaller and cosier sitting-room, than the somewhat formal drawing-room on the ground floor.

'Thank you, Carlton,' said his lordship, moving forward to stand in front of Grace, 'please see that we are not disturbed.'

The man withdrew and Grace looked up into the stern face of Lord Jaspar Ede. She gave a small sigh and thought that she had never seen a more sensible, intelligent and pleasing countenance before.

'I am *so* glad to see you,' she said.

'Well, well,' remarked Lord Jaspar, surveying her from his great height, 'what brings you to London, Miss Grace? And why to me? I thought you never wanted to see me again, and that you would be safely and determinedly married to the country bumpkin of your choice?'

'I need your help desperately,' cried Grace. 'Everything has gone wrong and I am not married, but Lord Pridmont has taken Sammy away and unless I promise to marry him I shall never see my son again. *Please* help me to get him back!'

Lord Jaspar blinked. 'I am not hearing right,' he said. 'Lord Pridmont wishes to *marry* you?'

'Yes.' Grace shifted the baby in her arms and took a deep breath. 'I know that sounds incredible but it is the truth, and I *cannot* marry that devil, and I have run away and Richard Mercury is searching for me and when he doesn't find me he'll go back to Lord Pridmont and then — ' she stopped and gave a sob of anguish — 'then they'll hurt Sammy to punish me, and you *must* save him, oh, please, you must!'

'Steady on.' Lord Jaspar put a hand beneath her elbow and drew her towards the sofa. 'Sit down there and calm yourself. I do not understand a word of all this, but no doubt clarity will emerge in due course. Now why, for heaven's sake, should Pridmont offer you marriage? And why should you not agree?'

Grace's mouth fell open and she stared up at her companion in horror. 'I would not let him touch me! He only wants to marry me so that he can do with me what he wants. And he is old and revolting and uses Mercury to — to carry out — ' she stopped talking and burst into tears. 'He is a dreadful man,' she wailed, 'and so is that Richard Mercury, and they have stolen my Sammy and if you do not help me I don't know what will become of us all!'

Grace lowered her head and sobbed great, racking sobs which shook her slender frame. The baby awoke and joined in, adding her voice to the uproar.

'Good gracious, stop that noise at once,' commanded Lord Jaspar, 'or I shall be accused of murder!'

'I hope you are! I hope the constable hears and comes to investigate and I shall tell him everything and maybe *he* will show some sign of human decency and help me in my distress.' Grace rocked backwards and forwards with tears streaming down her face, as she held Hope against her shoulder and rubbed her back. 'This is your daughter, and I suppose you'd like to see her in that household? Growing into womanhood in the home of a lecher? Learning every sinful and evil thing there is to know in life? Is that what you want for your child's future?'

'My daughter?' Jaspar Ede walked round to study Hope's red face which appeared over the top of Grace's shoulder. 'Why, of course she is,' he said in a voice of wonder, and bent his tall figure forward to peer at the baby. She stopped crying and stared solemnly back at the man. Very gently Ede put out a hand and the little girl's fist came up and grasped his forefinger. 'My daughter,' repeated Ede softly, 'what do you call her?'

'Hope,' said Grace, and a strange emotion stirred in her bruised heart. Maybe everything would be all right after all. She bent sideways and wiped her wet cheek against the baby's back. 'You once said that you would like me to be your mistress,' she said in a muffled voice, 'and I wanted to tell you that I will agree to that. I'll do anything to please you, if you will get Sammy back for me. I was foolish and proud before, sir, when you asked me, but much has happened since then and I will do anything you ask if you will help me now.'

Lord Jaspar made an odd clucking sound with his tongue and bent his head nearer to Hope.

'By Jove,' he said, 'she is smiling at me!'

Grace turned round on the sofa and faced him, setting Hope upon her knee. 'She is a beautiful baby and you are right to be proud of her. But I have another child, sir, and cannot rest until he is safe. Please do something for Sammy, and quickly, before something dreadful happens to him.'

'He is Pridmont's son.' Lord Jaspar straightened his long back and put his hands behind him. 'I have no claim to him, and how the devil can I take him away from his father?'

'He is *not* Lord Pridmont's son — he was sired by Richard Mercury. But he

270

has no interest in the child, neither of them have, they only want him in order to gain control over me. You could get him back, sir. You can do anything if you set your mind to it.'

Lord Jaspar shook his head and walked away from her to stare out of the window. 'What can I do?' he murmured. 'It is impossible.'

Anger began to burn in Grace's bosom, banishing her fear and worry. She had dared everything to come to this man, believing that he would aid her. She had offered herself to him, and had been prepared to do anything he asked if he would but save her son.

She thought of Tom Laster, and of her own father, both of whom had rejected her in her hour of need. Even Lord Jaspar had deserted her in the past.

Dear God, thought Grace, standing up abruptly and tightening her shawl around Hope's small, warm body, was no man to be trusted? Was a female to be forever disappointed and discarded in misfortune?

Very well, she thought violently, she would accept Lord Pridmont's offer. With both wealth and position at her command she would watch and wait for her opportunity. Then, when the old man died — he could not live for very much longer — then she would be his widow and would eventually come into her own.

'Where are you going?' Lord Jaspar's voice brought her to a halt by the door.

'I am going to Lord Pridmont.' Grace lifted her chin and stared defiantly back at the man. 'It is the only thing left for me to do.'

Ede strode forward frowning. 'You are not taking my daughter into his household. I cannot allow that.' His eyes went to Hope and then returned to Grace's strained face. 'You had better remain here and I'll go out and see what can be done.' Then Lord Jaspar smiled and put out a hand to touch the girl's tear-stained cheek. 'You have courage,' he said softly, 'one must admire that. And you made me a most generous offer which I think should be taken up. You will agree to be my mistress if I retrieve Sammy for you?'

Grace nodded, relief flooding through her tired body. If she were under Lord Jaspar's protection, then Lord Pridmont would not dare to harm her; both she and the children would be safe.

'But you must make certain that he understands,' she said. 'The children must be safe, too. You must make yourself responsible for us at all times.'

Jaspar Ede sighed. 'I cannot promise but will do my best. Meanwhile I'll give orders for a room to be prepared for you, then you can wash and rest. I may be some time.'

He went out, and Grace heard his voice as he spoke to the butler in the hall below.

10

Two hours later Grace was sitting in front of a fire in Lord Jaspar's spare bedroom, wrapped in a blanket, with one of the housemaids drying her hair. Hope lay in a little basket which Carlton had miraculously produced from somewhere, and Grace and her baby had been bathed and clad in clean garments.

Hope was swathed in a strange assortment of towels and shawls, and Grace was wearing a cambric nightgown which the maid had given her.

'It's plain and simple, m'm, but 'tis clean, and Mister Carlton, 'e said 'twould do nicely.' She had bobbed and blinked in some confusion and Grace had smiled quickly to ease the girl's embarrassment.

'I am very grateful. Annie, isn't it?'

'Yes, m'm.' Another bob, and a

ducking of her neat capped head.

'I shall be sending for my own clothes tomorrow, but this will do beautifully for tonight. Thank you very much.'

Annie stood behind her, brushing Grace's hair in long slow strokes down her back. 'It is nearly dry now, m'm, and then you'd best to bed. Mister Carlton, 'e said you'd be weary and ready for your sleep, like.'

'I am tired, but I wish to hear news of Lord Jaspar. He — he is doing some business for me and I cannot sleep until he comes.'

The maid put down the brush and gave another little bob before going to the door. 'If there is anything you want just ring, m'm.'

Grace thanked her, then turned her gaze back to the fire as the door closed behind Annie.

She was almost asleep, dozing against her will, when she heard voices somewhere in the house below. Grace lifted her head with a jerk and listened intently. A while later there were swift, firm footsteps along the corridor outside and then a sharp rap on the door.

'Come in.' Grace was on her feet, clutching the blanket about her body with nervous fingers.

The door opened and Lord Jaspar strode forward with Sammy in his arms.

'You've found him!' Grace sprang towards him, the blanket slipping to the floor, and held out her arms for the boy. 'Sammy, oh, Sammy, thank God you're safe!'

'Mam!' he stretched out for her and as she reached him his hands went round her neck and he buried his face in her shoulder.

'There, there, my bunting, you are safe and sound with Mama. And you are never going away again, you hear me?'

She carried him back to the chair and seated herself upon it, cuddling the boy on her lap.

Lord Jaspar stood gazing down at

them. 'That's a pleasant sight,' he remarked, 'the poor little devil has been scared stiff with first Pridmont, and then me, laying hold of him. He'll be all right now, though, won't he?'

'He'll be all right.' Grace held Sammy firmly against her and kissed the top of his head. 'How did you do it?' She looked up at Ede with shining eyes. 'I shall never be able to thank you enough. How did you manage to get him away?'

Lord Jaspar walked to the fire and gazed down into the flames. 'I — er — exchanged you,' he said at last. 'Barter, if you like. I had something Pridmont wanted, and he had something *I* wanted, so the most sensible thing to do was exchange one for the other.'

He turned and looked at Grace, and at the drowsy, clinging figure of the boy; he studied her mass of coppery hair, shining clean and fragrant in the candlelight. He noticed the dark smudges beneath her eyes, and the drawn look to her mouth which had not been there when he had first seen her in London. Her face had lost the round-ness of youth, and her eyes were wiser, her mouth harder. But the beauty of her face had not diminished; indeed, it had strengthened and taken on an increased charm since she had experi-enced sorrow and disillusionment.

Lord Jaspar Ede looked at the parson's daughter, whose virtue he had destroyed, and felt that he had never desired her so much as at this moment when, tired but triumphant, she held Sammy close, wearing a starched cotton nightgown on her slender form.

'What did you exchange?' she asked a little fearfully. Was it very important to him? An object of great value? Some-thing which he would regret losing in time? 'I'll make it up to you. I promise to do whatever you ask of me. I shall not refuse you, nor nag, nor be impertinent.'

Lord Jaspar smiled. 'Do not promise too much, my dear Grace, or you will regret it. I cannot believe that you will not lose your temper with me ere long. You are not made to be calm and placid and dull, my sweet.'

Grace flushed at his mocking tone. 'I shall try not to become angry,' she said stiffly. 'I can promise to *try*, at least.'

'Yes, indeed,' said his lordship.

'Mam?' Sammy lifted his head. 'Mam? Home now?'

'Yes,' answered Lord Jaspar, bending forward and putting his hand on the boy's curly head. 'You are home now, Sammy, and can stay here for ever. Do you think you and Hope are going to like it in my house?'

The boy nodded gravely, looking up into the man's intent face.

'Don't,' whispered Grace, 'don't lie. I shall always speak the truth to my children, and we'll never hide behind lies and deceit. I've had enough of them in my life. Sammy, darling,' she bent her head over the boy's, and her hair enfolded him like curtains of silk. 'We are only staying here for a little while, and then kind Lord Ede is going to give us a home of our own — '

'I said he was home and I meant it.' Lord Jaspar's tone was sharp. 'This is your home, and you and the children will remain here with me.'

'But that is not right!' Grace exclaimed, lifting her head and shaking back her hair. 'You cannot have your mistress living with you, as well as her children. Why, it is not done, sir!'

'And what do you know about etiquette and what is, and is not, allowed in society, may I ask?'

Grace blushed again and then frowned. How dare he speak to her like that!

'I think we should discuss this later when I have put Sammy to bed.' She stood up abruptly. 'If you will leave us for a few minutes, sir, I'll give him a quick wash and — '

'And then you'll join me in the drawing-room? In your nightgown? Fie, ma'am, what goings on, to be sure! I thought you knew what was right and proper?' He shook his head at her.

Grace's eyes flashed and she bit her lip to restrain the words she longed to say. Dear heavens, but he was infuriating! How could she ever keep her temper when he riled her so?

'Come, Grace, I'm only teasing.' Lord Jaspar moved forward and took Sammy from her. 'Here, my lad, let's wash your face and hands in this basin and then we'll tumble you into bed. Tomorrow we'll go out and buy you a fine set of new clothes to wear, what say you to that, eh, Samuel?'

The little boy smiled and gave the man a small, fierce hug.

'That's woman's work!' cried Grace in amazement, as Lord Jaspar carried the child over to the washstand and then put him down and splashed water somewhat awkwardly over the boy's face.

'If he is to by my son I shall start learning now. It is time he and I became better acquainted.' Soap was rubbed into Sammy's palms and then each fist was plunged into the bowl of water. 'Now the towel, there, that's a good lad.'

'Your son?' Grace sank down upon the edge of the bed, her forehead creased in puzzlement. 'Please explain to me what is going on, I do not understand anything.'

'Now, off with your shoes, here, let me.' Lord Jaspar swung the boy onto the bed beside Grace, and began removing first one shoe and then the other.

'The truth of the matter is, dear Grace, that I am about to make an honest woman of you. No, do not speak, you told me that I could do with you what I would, so remain silent, if you please.' As he spoke, Lord Jaspar continued to undress Sammy, slowly and clumsily, until the child was peeled to his under garments. 'There, into bed with you. Mama will join you in a few minutes.'

His lordship straightened and looked at Grace with amused eyes. 'I am going to marry you, sweet, and adopt this young man — give him my name — so we'll be a proper family from the beginning.'

'But — but you never wanted me before!' Grace stared in bewilderment.

'Wrong! I wanted you always, but it was not until Pridmont decided to wed you that I realised what a very good idea that was. As Pridmont so rightly said, as a *wife* you would be totally controlled and, of course, protected. So, as Lady Ede, no one will dare to harm one hair of your lovely head, ma'am, and both you and the children will be safe, as you so earnestly requested.'

'I cannot believe it. Are you certain this is what you want? Is it a *sensible* thing to do, sir?' Grace put a hand to her brow. 'I am not well-born, I might disgrace you — oh, have you thought about it enough?'

Lord Jaspar moved forward and took her hands in his. For once his eyes were serious. 'I have thought about little else since I left you in such dire fashion all those months ago. I mean, when our baby was conceived, dear heart. I realised to my horror and shame that you had been speaking the truth about your innocence, and I was so filled with disgust and self-loathing, Grace, that I ran away to try and ease my conscience.

'But I could not forget you, nor what I had done to you, and so I came back to England in order to find you. But I still only wanted you as my mistress. Being a confirmed bachelor, I intended remaining so until my death.'

Grace lifted her chin and Lord Jaspar put out a gentle hand and tapped her face with his knuckles. 'What a fool I was! Such courage, and so much beauty and intelligence, all to be thrown away on a country bumpkin, or so I believed. But now, God willing, all has come right in the end. I have seen the folly of my ways and we can begin all over again. Will you, my dear Miss Fairweather, marry me?'

'I think I had better,' she replied. 'So

much has gone wrong in my life until now, but there is nothing I would rather be than your wife.'

'Then that is settled.' Lord Jaspar bent and kissed her quickly on the mouth. Then he stepped back and looked away from her eager, happy face. 'Now I shall depart before I disgrace myself and teach young Samuel things he'd be better learning when he is some years older.'

'What,' said Grace, trying to control her voice, for Ede's embrace had awakened a desire in her which had lain dormant for the past twelve months, 'what did you exchange for me and Sammy? You never told me.'

'Oh,' said his lordship, swinging round from the door, 'I forgot to say. I exchanged you for that painting of nymphs and things.'

'Not the Boucher?' exclaimed Grace in awe.

Lord Jaspar Ede nodded. 'Pridmont has always wanted it to add to his collection, and as I am now to have my own goddess I saw no reason why he should not possess a canvas version.'

Grace smiled, her grey eyes brimming with unshed tears. 'Thank you,' she whispered.

'You can thank me properly in a few weeks time when the banns have been called,' said his lordship hurriedly, and left the room whilst he still had the determination to behave in a right and proper manner.

THE END

We do hope that you have enjoyed reading this large print book.

Did you know that all of our titles are available for purchase?

We publish a wide range of high quality large print books including:
**Romances, Mysteries, Classics
General Fiction
Non Fiction and Westerns**

Special interest titles available in large print are:
**The Little Oxford Dictionary
Music Book, Song Book
Hymn Book, Service Book**

Also available from us courtesy of Oxford University Press:
**Young Readers' Dictionary
(large print edition)
Young Readers' Thesaurus
(large print edition)**

For further information or a free brochure, please contact us at:
**Ulverscroft Large Print Books Ltd.,
The Green, Bradgate Road, Anstey,
Leicester, LE7 7FU, England.
Tel:** (00 44) **0116 236 4325
Fax:** (00 44) **0116 234 0205**

Other titles in the
Linford Romance Library:

THE ECHOING BELLS

Lillie Holland

In Germany Marnie Burness accepts the post of governess at Schloss Beissel. Her charge is Count von Oldenburg's daughter, Charlotte. Despite finding much to disapprove of at the Schloss, against her own principles she falls in love with the Count. Then, when Maria, the Count's wife, is murdered Marnie suspects his involvement. She leaves the Schloss, but will she ever learn the truth about the death of the countess — and will her suspicions of the Count be proved right?